About the author

Paul Youden began his career in journalism in 1957 with a 5-year apprenticeship with the *Kent Messenger*, and attended journalism college for four years. Once qualified, he became a senior journalist with the *Kentish Express*, rising to County News Editor. He then worked for BBC Radio (South East) and was headhunted by the Port of Dover where, from 1975, he was in charge of press, PR and marketing. He remained there for twenty years, rising to Corporate Affairs Manager, but took early retirement in the 1990s to return to full-time writing, producing travel books on motoring and skiing for Vauxhall Motors for eight years, after which he set up his own travel website.

With his wife's terminal illness, he had to give up many of his travels and cut back on his writing, but decided in 2014 – prompted by his wife's illness – to attempt his first novel: *The Powder Man*. He is currently working on the sequel.

THE POWDER MAN

Paul Youden

Book Guild Publishing

First published in Great Britain in 2015 by
The Book Guild Ltd
9 Priory Business Park
Kibworth, LE8 0RX

Copyright © Paul Youden 2015

The right of Paul Youden to be identified as the author of
this work has been asserted by him in accordance with the
Copyright, Designs and Patents Act 1988.

All rights reserved. No part of this publication may be reproduced,
transmitted, or stored in a retrieval system, in any form
or by any means, without permission in writing from the publisher,
nor be otherwise circulated in any form of binding or cover other than
that in which it is published and without a similar condition being
imposed on the subsequent purchaser.

All characters in this publication are fictitious and any resemblance to
real people, alive or dead, is purely coincidental.

Typesetting in Garamond by
Ellipsis Digital Ltd, Glasgow

Printed and bound in Great Britain by
CPI Group (UK) Ltd, Croydon, CR0 4YY

A catalogue record for this book is available from
The British Library.

ISBN 978 1 910508 94 7

1

Was it Really all Worthwhile?

It was just like any other Monday in the editorial office: the editor closeted with his news editor and chief reporter, planning the day and hoping against hope that a really good story would break instead of yet another political lead from local council meetings or something from the weekly magistrates' court. Peter Kingston sat there at his computer trying to breathe some glamour, and even humour, into the dreary report of the Saturday Christmas bazaar at the town hall. Peter always felt that Christmas bazaars in November were something of a misnomer, and were the Women's Institute cakes really important enough to warrant even a paragraph of copy? But then the president was the wife of the mayor and the editor always insisted on coverage for the worshipful partnership.

Peter's mind was not really on what he was writing. His trouble was daydreaming, drifting off to a world where his ambition to travel would suddenly be realised: perhaps a win on the premium bonds, perhaps even his lottery gamble would produce five or even six numbers instead of the one or two, which was usually the case when he checked them on a Saturday evening. Peter's life was certainly in a rut and yet it seemed to have held such high promise when he passed out of The Journalists' College, Canterbury, after three years of hard work, sweat and sometimes tears. His marks had been high; his course tutor had praised his 'natural ability as a writer'. Even his editor, Bert Maynard, had remarked on Peter's ability to 'sniff out and produce' a good story. That was two years ago and how far forward was he? Peter was reduced to scanning the ads in the Journalist Journal each week to see if the right opening to suit his ambition was being advertised. So far he had found nothing; yet he had to question why he remained where he was. Certainly, the paper was paying him top whack for his age and ability, but Peter was sure the editor realised he had itchy feet. Peter had even dropped the right hint whenever the opportunity presented itself. He didn't want to be known just as a good court or council reporter; he didn't simply want front page bylines (although he had achieved those on more than one occasion during the last two years). No, what he really wanted was to travel, even to become a good travel writer. But the opportunity never seemed to present itself.

Peter Kingston came from a sound, middle-class family, but he had never wanted to go into the family firm. Working in an estate agency seemed even more mundane than what he was currently doing. His father always insisted on him getting a good education and finding a sound career; he never missed an opportunity to remind Peter that hard work, loyalty and dedication brought rewards of advancement to those who were prepared to be patient.

Peter's mother knew of his ambition to travel but constantly reminded Peter not to needle his father about quitting his job on the paper. After all, hadn't his father reminded him of the numerous unemployed these days and how grateful he should be in having a good home and a secure job?

Peter had enjoyed a number of girlfriends; the best had probably been Sue, who had been at the journalists' college at the same time. She had been warm, loving and had been his first relationship. It had been pure bliss and Sue had taught him how to be tender and patient.

'Sex is something to be savoured, much like a good wine,' she had always insisted. She was also always ready to listen to his dreams of distant travel. Sue had even gone as far as to suggest that they might form a partnership once they qualified. Then she was offered a job on a London fashion magazine and they drifted apart. They did occasionally keep in touch and Peter sometimes bought a copy of Sue's magazine to see what articles she had been writing. But then Melissa came on the scene. She worked at the local council offices and lived in a small, two-roomed flat on the outskirts of town. She really didn't have any great ambitions, although she agreed that Peter should strive to become a good travel writer. Yet it always seemed to Peter, as they snuggled up on the sofa in front of her realistic, log-burning, gas fire, that Melissa just wanted to find somebody to settle down with and be a stay-at-home mum. That was not his vision for the next five years or so, nor was living at home at the age of 24 with his mother, constantly nagging him about all things unnecessary, his father constantly reminding him that hard work and loyalty always stood a person in good stead for the future.

The opening of the editor's door, loud voices and the clatter of feet on the stairs brought Peter's mind back into the reality of the moment.

'Peter!' boomed the voice of Dave Edwards, the rather 'I-fancy-myself' news editor. 'Have you finished that report yet? There are a couple of pics to go with it so it might make a page.'

A page, thought Peter to himself. *If I were in charge, it might warrant a couple of paras at best.*

'Nearly, Dave!' Peter called back.

'Well, be quick about it. I want you down at the magistrates' court. It looks as if we have a hit and run case from yesterday and the chap's in quite a bad way. It's possible that the driver might have been drinking, although when the police picked him up this morning, it was too late to produce a positive breath test.'

Great! thought Peter to himself then, out loud, he replied, 'I'll get onto it right away, Dave.' He looked at his watch – 9.35 a.m. Just time to ring the desk sergeant at the local nick and see if he could glean any more information. After that, he could call Carol at the magistrates' clerks' office; she was always helpful and perhaps sometimes gave Peter too much information. Not that Peter minded; he liked Carol but didn't want her getting into trouble with her boss and his valuable source of info drying up.

John Drysdale was the desk sergeant who had never quite made inspector. He was one of the old school of policemen: not enough grey matter for the likes of modern policing and the wet-behind-the-ears guys who came straight from police training college onto the street with the rank of inspector just because they held a university degree. No, John Drysdale was a real cop who had worked his way up from a beat policeman in the days when they still had policemen on the streets.

'John, it's Peter from the Surrey Chronicle. I've got to attend this alleged hit and run case and I was wondering if there might be a few details you could fill me in with, off the record, if I popped in on my way to the magistrates' court?'

'Now you know better than to ask me that,' said Sergeant John in his usual public voice, as no doubt somebody was listening in the background. 'But if you call in, I'll ask the inspector just how much is going to come out in court. Of course, it's only a preliminary hearing and I expect the police will be asking for a remand in custody.'

Peter thanked John and knew there would be some help forthcoming; might even make a few lines for their sister paper, *News Now*, which was published daily and although 80% of its contents were national stories, it sold well on a regional basis throughout Kent. Before leaving the office, Peter called Carol and asked if there was any chance of having the name of the vehicle driver or his victim. Unusually, Carol wasn't forthcoming.

'It's all a bit difficult, Peter. If I could help, you know I would, but things are a bit awkward at the moment.'

Peter said thanks anyway and hung up. It was certainly not like Carol. If her boss had been hovering, she would have gone into a pre-rehearsed line about cooking dinner or, yes, she would love to go to the cinema.

As Peter left the office for the half-mile walk through the town to the court building, via the police station, he was still uncertain about Carol's slightly off-handed answer. *Never mind; better luck with Sergeant John.* But there wasn't. The police sergeant, although he secretly admired Peter for his down to earth and honest approach to journalism, was really not at all helpful.

'Sorry, Peter, this one's a bit difficult. I think you'd better wait for the court case. You know I would help you if I could but orders have been issued from on high. No help to the press at this stage . . . even to our local friends!'

What on earth could be going on? Peter was even more puzzled. It was the first time he had encountered such a barrier of silence.

As he walked towards the court building, there was an unusual degree of activity: some chaps with cameras, a film crew setting up and obviously some out-of-town reporters. You could spot them, even smell them, from a distance; something to do with the drinking and smoking, no doubt, on the London dailies. Peter had heard so much about this while at journalists' college at Canterbury from one of the tutors, a former Fleet Street reporter, and it had really put him off trying to start out his career in the big time.

As he made his way into the magistrates' court building, he had to struggle to get a seat on the press bench.

'Who's he?' Peter heard a voice from the end of the row.

'Don't know,' came the reply. 'Probably some local scribe who thinks he's about to make the big time,' said the scruffy-looking bloke in the tatty-looking, black leather jacket sitting next to him.

Peter ignored both and settled himself down with his notebook and pen. He realised he had absolutely no details yet. Suggested hit-and-run: so why the interest from the nationals? Did his editor and Dave know more than they were willing to let on when they came out of this morning's meeting?

There was a commotion behind him. Peter looked round, as did the other eight reporters sitting alongside him, to see the driver charged with the offence: a middle-aged, bearded man in handcuffs, flanked by two policemen.

'All rise,' said the court usher as the magistrate appeared. Peter was surprised to see that the chairman of the bench, no less, was taking the case. It was quite a rarity for Graham Blackman, president of the local Rotary Club, a senior member of the town council and tipped as a future mayor. Everyone did a slight bow or nod and waited until the magistrate was seated before they settled back on the uncomfortable press bench. Peter had quickly noticed quite a few people in the public gallery and they were not faces he immediately recognised or associated with locals.

The clerk rose to read the charge. 'On Sunday the twenty-fifth of November, you, Nigel Ewell, did fail to stop after . . .'

Peter did not hear the remainder. Now it all fitted into place. No wonder the wall of silence. Nigel Ewell had been on the run for months after evading arrest at Dover on drug-smuggling charges. Nigel Ewell, the notorious 'Powder Man' of the drugs underworld, who had been the subject of much press speculation in recent months; he had even been linked to a number of unresolved murders by a national BBC television programme. Now things started to fit into place.

Peter's attention was quickly brought back to the proceedings by the booming voice of Chief Superintendent Tom Crowthall, asking for a remand in custody as other matters of a more serious nature were currently being investigated.

'I must protest most strongly,' said the solicitor, obviously acting for Nigel Ewell. 'My client vigorously denies the charge before the court and was nowhere near the vicinity of the alleged incident yesterday. Naturally, he offers his sincere sympathy to the relatives of the injured victim, but as he was not driving the vehicle or near the scene, I am instructed to ask for his immediate release from custody.'

Chief Superintendent Crowthall was back on his feet, reminding the magistrate that the offence of failing to stop following a road accident was serious in itself. However, he would remind the court that Nigel Ewell was wanted elsewhere by other authorities on even more serious charges and until investigations were completed, he must insist as strongly as possible for a remand in custody. The police and other authorities felt there was a real danger of Mr Ewell going abroad.

Graham Blackman lent across the bench, his clerk rose with his back to the court and there were several minutes of mutterings. The clerk turned, sat down and the chairman of the bench announced, 'Nigel Ewell, I have decided, in view of the seriousness of this offence and other matters pending, to remand you in custody for seven days.'

The clerk said, 'All rise,' and Graham Blackman bowed, turned and left the bench. There then followed a mad scramble of reporters trying to push past Peter, who was still trying to take it all in. *Here in our town, an international criminal, remanded pending further investigations?* Certainly front page stuff, but by the time Peter's own weekly was out, the news would have been splashed worldwide. And in any event, 'matters of a more serious nature' were not of real interest to the people of Tonbridge. What really mattered now was who had been knocked down and how badly they were hurt.

As the Fleet Street scribes crackled words down their mobile phones (oh, how Peter hated mobile phones, always going off at the wrong time: in the cinema, in a restaurant and once he even heard one bleeping during a wedding in church), Peter walked briskly back to his newspaper office. Dave was waiting and by now Peter realised he had known more than he had previously let on.

'Well, Peter, I think you and I had better go and see the boss. Be prepared to get a few paragraphs hurriedly written for *News Now*. They go to press within the hour and we can steal a march on the London evening papers at the very least.'

Peter and Dave went through the glass-panelled door into Bert Maynard's office and sat down.

'Quite a turn up for our town,' said Bert, a middle-aged man with a paunch from drinking too much beer and with facial skin not helped by excessive smoking. 'Quite an opportunity for you, Peter. I want you to see this one through. Take one of the juniors with you to help with the extra legwork. This story could turn out quite big next time our man Ewell appears in the dock. But for now, get a few column inches off to our sister daily and then set about finding out who the victim of the hit and run is and anything else you can about the accident.'

Peter got up, turned and left without comment, but was inwardly full of hope that this was finally something for him to sink his teeth into.

Peter phoned his story through to the copy taker at *News Now* and looked at his watch. 12.10 p.m. The morning had flown by. Just time to map out his follow-up story for his own paper, grab a sandwich at the Ugly Duckling pub across the road and then he would take junior reporter, Andrew Forsythe, out for a real taste of legwork.

Peter called across the room to where Andrew was sitting. 'Give me a minute of your time, Andrew!'

Andrew sauntered over, hands in pockets and obviously yet to learn that senior reporters were to be respected and listened to.

'You're going to assist me on this hit and run case,' said Peter in his most assertive of voices. 'Orders from the editor no less, but from now on you take your directions from me. There will be a lot of legwork, some phoning and no swanning off at five o'clock today. We will be seeing this through to the bitter end,' said Peter, at last looking up and facing Andrew eye to eye.

Andrew got the message. His face portrayed an awareness and recognition of sound advice from a more senior and mature as well as highly respected colleague.

Peter told him that he would be back within thirty minutes by which time he would like some thoughts on how he, Andrew, would follow up the story. 'It will be good training for you, perhaps the sort of question you might get in next year's exams at college. And no doubt the editor will want a report from me on your future potential,' said Peter, forcing a slight smile and winking at Andrew.

He left the office, walked into the pub and Dorothy, who always displayed too much of what she had above the waistline, said, 'Usual, Peter? And we have some very nice homemade steak and kidney pie and chips today.'

Peter said that would do him fine, but he was in a bit of a rush. He found himself a table in a quiet corner, got out his notebook and began mapping out the afternoon's work: time of accident, place of accident, name of victim, condition of victim, who was presumably still in the district hospital, any clues as to what Nigel Ewell might have been doing in Tonbridge. Peter's list got longer and suddenly, there was Dorothy with his beer and pie, bending over and letting Peter know that the pie was not the only delicious item on her menu.

'Dreadful business that accident,' said Dorothy, who was never slow in picking up local gossip. 'I hear the driver's got a long list of previous convictions,' she added, obviously trying to pump Peter for more info.

'Wouldn't know,' said Peter in a rather casual way. 'I think my story for Friday is likely to centre on the poor victim, whoever she or he may be. I don't suppose you know who the person is, do you?'

Dorothy shrugged. 'I heard it was some bloke from out of town but then I'm usually the last person to hear,' she said.

Peter didn't comment. Coming from Dorothy, he thought that rather rich, but as she was often a valuable source of news for him, he didn't want to provoke an argument. Besides, time was marching on and he wanted to finish his meal quickly.

After he had eaten, he made his way back to the newspaper office and the editorial room was empty except for Andrew.

'Well?' asked Peter, walking across the room. 'Where do you think we should start?'

Andrew looked up and smiled with a slight smirk. 'I thought you wouldn't mind but as you were off having a bite to eat, I took the initiative and phoned my sister who, as you know, is a nurse at the district hospital. She was on casualty early this morning when the accident victim was brought in: chap in his mid-thirties, two broken legs, broken arm, probably has some internal injuries and is still unconscious. More than her life was worth to give me a name. But, interestingly, she did say the chap was in intensive care with a policeman outside the door.' As he finished his speech, Andrew looked pleased with himself.

Peter was quietly impressed but didn't let on. No point in

over-inflating Andrew's ego at this stage. 'Yes, well, that's not a bad start, but I would like you to clear all moves with me first.'

Peter told Andrew that he should try and find the identity of the car involved, speak to Chief Superintendent Crowthall and see what else might be forthcoming. 'I think there's more to this case than meets the eye, so I'm going to see if I can find out the identity of the crash victim. I'm sure the police will have wanted to find relatives,' said Peter as he started to leave the office. Then Dave called him over to his news editor's desk.

'Peter, I've just heard that the victim was no less than our own Bob Hoskins, chief "No" crime reporter for *News Now*. What on earth he was doing here in Tonbridge in the early hours is anyone's guess. It seems too much of a coincidence that the alleged driver is the most wanted drugs man in Britain and he runs over one of the best investigative crime reporters I have ever known. See if his family can be more helpful.'

Peter left the office. This case was getting more baffling by the minute. Perhaps Dave was right; it all seemed too much of a coincidence.

Later that afternoon, he read through the day's edition of *News Now*. His story from the court case was a straightforward two paragraphs and only mentioning the name of Nigel Ewell as being the alleged driver who was wanted in connection with other matters. *News Now* had added their own paragraph, confirming the victim as being the paper's reporter, Bob Hoskins.

That evening, Peter curled up in front of Melissa's fire, mulling over the events of the day. There was little he could write about as it was mainly *sub judice* and pure speculation. He needed to switch off but found it difficult. Was there a definite link between Nigel Ewell and Bob Hoskins? Bob was a steady enough fellow. Perhaps he was following up a lead. But it was too much of a coincidence that he should get run over by this big-time criminal. And the police were still not saying how they had come to apprehend Nigel Ewell following the hit and run crash.

Melissa came into the room with a mug of hot chocolate and a malt whisky. It was Peter's favourite night-time tipple.

'Get this down you and stop worrying. Relax,' she said as she snuggled up alongside him wearing little beneath her dressing gown. 'Tomorrow's another day, Peter. You must learn to relax more.'

Peter had heard it all before and in any event, he wasn't really in the mood for lovemaking, always one of Melissa's evening priorities. She caressed his temple, nibbled his ear and made slight humming noises, always a sure sign she was warming to more positive things.

'Melissa, I really don't think I can tonight. This case is really troubling me and I must get on top of the story in the morning. It's a real chance to make a mark with the editor. So I'll finish my drink and sleep at home tonight. Give my parents a shock to see me sleeping in my own bed for a change.' Peter gave Melissa a passionate kiss, promised he would be on better form the following night, slipped on his black, leather jacket and quickly waved goodbye from her flat door before she could protest too much.

The following morning, Peter was summoned to a conference with the editor and Dave Edwards.

'We're going to have to play this one fairly straight,' said Bert. 'I have had word from the editor-in-chief on *News Now* that they regard the follow-up court case from here on in as their story. Sorry, Peter. Still, you can write something for us. I'm sure another story will come along that you can really get your teeth into.'

Peter left feeling decidedly unhappy. This had really been his chance to get involved in something big. It was typical of the big boys at *News Now* to want to hog all the copy themselves. Still, he would not let things rest. He could still make some enquiries himself and see what the connection was between Bob Hoskins and Nigel Ewell, if indeed there was one.

The rest of the week passed in a fairly mundane way. Peter went to the full meeting of the council, but typically, most of the controversial discussions had taken place in committee and the press were always excluded when it suited councillors – or indeed officials. The full council meeting usually rubber-stamped committee work unless elections were pending and certain councillors wanted to make a name for themselves by raking up dirt and thus ensure they had their names in the weekly paper. Peter was not impressed. After all, most councillors were in it for their own gratification and really couldn't care less about the voters.

He was just putting the finishing touches to a couple of articles when Dave Edwards called him over.

'Not much space left now, Peter. Probably worth holding over a few things for next week's paper. It will probably be your article on an extension to the town centre car parking ban and hefty increases in parking charges at the multi-story that will make front page lead. I'm sure the councillors simply want to drive shoppers and visitors to out of town complexes.'

Peter made his way over to the Ugly Duckling for some lunch. Dorothy was in her usual 'fancy that' mood.

'I hear it was one of your own reporters that got knocked over, Peter. Just shows, even journalists are not immune from getting knocked off their perches once in a while.'

Peter was not in the mood for subtle sarcasm. He mumbled, 'I expect you're right,' and sat in his usual corner with half a shandy and waited for his chicken curry.

A few minutes later, Andrew Forsythe popped in.

'Thought I might find you in here, Peter. Word has it there's been a development in the Ewell case and HM Customs have asked the DPP for the case to be switched to London. Looks as if our own hit and run takes second place to the drugs affair.'

Peter wasn't really listening. After all, he wasn't on the case anymore and it let him off the hook slightly, in the eyes of his colleagues, if the case was switched away from Tonbridge to the Old Bailey.

When he got back to the office, Dave informed Peter of what he had recently heard from Andrew then said, 'The editor's gone up to head office for some sort of meeting this afternoon about the whole affair. Seems Bob Hoskins is in a fairly serious way and is being moved to East Grinstead for specialist treatment.'

Peter nodded and made a non-committal reply then made his way over to his desk. What a way to earn a living: mundane court and council meetings, Christmas bazaars. Just about to get his teeth into a good story and the rug's pulled from under his feet. Were the four years at college and his five-year apprenticeship really worthwhile? At this moment in time, he doubted it. 'There must be something better out there for me somewhere,' sighed Peter to himself.

2

Ready For Christmas

It was Monday morning, 17th December. Peter had managed to do most of his Christmas shopping. His parents were inviting friends for Christmas Day. His sister was coming over with her brood: three kids, all totally out of hand, and a husband who purported to be a research scientist but looked more like a twentieth-century hippy. Money wise, Julie had landed on her feet and of course, Daddy was thrilled.

'There you are, Peter. A good, settled home, nice income; what more could a person want?'

A lot more, thought Peter. And certainly no kids, unruly or otherwise, screeching around the house.

The editorial meeting had just ended. Unusually, John Riddell, the editor-in-chief from head office, had sat in on the discussions. *Must be something up*, thought Peter to himself. At that moment, Peter was summoned to Bert Maynard's office.

'I think you've met our editor-in-chief, Peter,' said Bert.

'Yes, nice to see you again, Peter,' said the plumpish, bespectacled John Riddell. 'Now, Peter, this sorry business of last week involving Bob Hoskins . . . He's going to be out of action for some time, months maybe, so I have had to make some changes at head office, move a few people round to take over fresh responsibilities. I don't expect you will be surprised to learn that I keep an eye on my boys with potential and Bert here reinforces my view that you have a solid future in journalism and hopefully it will remain with our group.'

Peter nodded agreement. Where on earth was all this leading? Promotion to head office? He hoped not; he rather liked the Tonbridge lifestyle, but then could he afford to turn down an opportunity?

'Bert tells me you have an interest in travel; it's certainly the up and coming pastime. More spending power, more free time. Everyone wants to go somewhere but the information they glean from travel agents usually leaves a lot to be desired. So it is my intention to start a series on travel. It may be weekly; it may be more frequent. Depends on what the advertising chappies feel they can get in the way of support income. So the deal is, Peter, I thought you might like to try your hand at writing a few articles. It's the start of the winter sports season, so we might as well start with that. Lots of people from the southeast, and especially our readership area, fancy themselves as the elite of the piste. I think that's the expression. Anyway, I want you to do a bit of research in the next couple of days, find out where most people go for winter sports and why. Draw me up a plan to be on my desk Friday. I think you can safely assume you will be away for Christmas and doing quite a bit of travelling in the New Year. No family commitments, no holiday plans so Bert informs me. Not good for an enthusiastic young journalist with potential to get himself tied down too much too early,' said John Riddell with a wry smile. 'Well, that's about it, Peter. It's now really up to you. Make a name for yourself with some good copy and a chance to specialise. Bert will discuss the details with you but don't forget a plan of action on my desk by first thing Friday morning.'

And with that, Peter left his editor's office, reeling from the news, unable to take it all in. He needed to talk to someone: not his parents, not Melissa, who wouldn't understand his deserting her. Perhaps he might give Sue a ring in London. After all, she was a girl of the world now and might give him a few pointers. Yes, that's what he would do and then he might have a celebratory drink at the Ugly Duckling. Strange how things suddenly moved; one minute, stuck in a rut and wondering if it was all worthwhile; next minute, given the opportunity to fulfil a lifelong ambition to travel – and getting paid for it into the bargain. Yes, he was certain he could make a good job of this opportunity.

Peter rang Sue's office. The woman at the other end of the phone explained that Sue was out on a picture shoot for some big London store.

'Leave me your name and I'll get her to call you when she comes in.'

Peter left his name and said he would be at the newspaper office number until 6.30 p.m. He just hoped Sue would ring back before then. He then called the local travel agents, part of a nationwide chain. The manager was in, so Peter explained he wanted some information on skiing, resorts and which countries were the most popular.

'Call round after lunch,' said the manager, 'and I will have dug out some brochures. We'll start there.'

That should be jolly, Peter thought to himself as he settled on 2.15 p.m. as a suitable time. Meanwhile, he just had time to finish that article left over from Wednesday's council meeting. Contractors had botched a job on a new sewer extension, resulting in the flooding of residents' gardens, leaving an almighty smell. *Well*, thought Peter, *pay peanuts and you get monkeys*. He remembered the council's director of environment – a fancy title with an equally fancy salary, plus car – singing the praises of this particular contractor. Now somebody would have to eat humble pie and the insurance company would be footing the bill, no doubt.

Peter had no time for lunch. He hurried down to the travel agents and true to his word, the manager had not only got out plenty of brochures, he had jotted down a few pointers.

'Doing some sort of travel piece, are we?' he enquired.

'Sort of,' retorted Peter, not wishing to divulge too much at this stage. 'Thought I would swot up on the subject.'

The manager said Europe was still the favourite with the majority of winter sports holidaymakers. 'We have a few who like to try America. There is some good skiing over there, but you're talking about long flights, long transfers and a very regimented mountain course. My company sent me on a fact-finding mission last winter and I was not overly impressed. The USA has tried to copy Europe by building some new, expensive resorts and putting in the latest hi-tech lift systems. Trouble is, the resorts lack the atmosphere that you find in countries like Switzerland and Austria.'

Peter did not know too much about European skiing resorts, but was surprised there had been no mention of France.

'Ah, you see,' said the travel agency manager, now warming to the situation. 'France has had a pretty poor snow record for a number of years now and they have been chasing the snow, building new concrete monstrosities — that's my view — higher and higher up mountains. There are even new complexes at more than two thousand metres. That's about six thousand six hundred feet in our terms. Big cable cars then transport guests to glacier regions and the poor old French village back down in the valley, once quite popular, has been left behind. No, you give me Switzerland and Austria for atmosphere. Might even include a few, but only a few, Italian resorts. Some in the Dolomites are still attracting Brits,' he continued.

Peter realised his research was going to include a geography session. Better get out the atlas and swot up on mountain regions.

'This is all extremely useful,' said Peter, aware that time was marching on and he wanted to get back in case Sue phoned. 'But how do people travel to the mountains? Fly, I suppose?'

'Some still do, some like this new Euro-train that leaves London every Friday evening and transports you direct to the Alps via the Channel Tunnel. But the train only goes to the French Alps and then only to a region known as the Tarentaise. No, the way to travel is by car.'

'By car!' exclaimed Peter. 'That must take days and what about all that snow on the roads? Must be a nightmare.'

'Quite the reverse. If you want to see a real winter, snow-clearing operation, drive through Europe. They've got it off to a tee. All the way to the resorts. They can't afford to have last week's guests snowed in, otherwise next week's guests have nowhere to stay,' he said with a wry grin.

Peter hadn't realised there was so much to this travel business. Did he know what he was letting himself in for? He would have to get on with his research in detail right away. After all, a plan of action had to be on the editor-in-chief's desk by Friday morning.

Peter hurried back to his office. No, Sue hadn't phoned. He was disappointed. Perhaps she wasn't interested anymore; the high life of London was probably her scene now with dozens of potential boyfriends snapping at her heels. He pored over the numerous tour operators' brochures; he hadn't appreciated so many tour companies were chasing winter sports enthusiasts. There was more to this snow business than he realised. Eventually, he decided to make a list: who went where, how people travelled, most popular duration of holiday. There even appeared to be special arrangements for kids. Yes, that was a great story: kids, or most of them, loved snow. There was a good angle there to follow up.

When his list was complete, it seemed more like the introduction to a book and he would have to summarise it. And, gosh, was that the time? 6.10 p.m. The afternoon had flown by.

The phone rang.

'Hello,' said Peter, his mind still on travel thoughts.

'Hi, Peter. It's Sue. Remember me, from your dim and distant past?' she said with a faint chuckle down the line. 'I thought it must be important if you were phoning me after all these months. Missed me or do you want something?'

'Both,' said Peter. 'Look, I'd rather not go into detail over the phone, so can we arrange to meet soonest? I need to pick your brains and to remind myself just how lovely a girl I've let slip though the net.'

Sue retorted, 'Peter Kingston, you are a big flatterer and if you think you've let me through that net of yours, you can't have much regard for yourself. I might want to see you just to let you know that I haven't forgotten you completely, even if I am permanently in the big city.'

Peter asked Sue if she was busy that evening. 'It really is important to me to bounce some ideas off you, Sue. I expect you have a date and will tell me it's impossible,' he said in a rather dispirited voice.

'Oh, come on, Peter. Don't put on that hard-done-by act for me. Remember, it's Sue you're talking to. I know you of old. Anyway, yes, I do have a date tonight. I was out on a picture shoot for the magazine for most of the day and the client invited me to join *her* and some other people. So you see, it's not a *him* and not because you sound so disconsolate but because it would be lovely to see you again, the answer is yes, I'd love to. But it won't be until about half eight. Where do you want to meet?'

Peter said he would drive to her flat at Chiswick, providing that was convenient. They could go for a meal somewhere.

'Just get yourself to my place; it's ages since I had the chance to cook for somebody I really liked. But bring a bottle of Merlot. I'm right out of wine and if I remember correctly, we share the same taste in red wine.'

Peter was thrilled. It was all too much: the chance of a new career opening before him, providing he worked hard at it, renewing a close friendship with Sue (at least he hoped it would be close) and the only thing left to do was telephone his parents and say he had a business meeting in town. He could tell them the rest tomorrow. He certainly couldn't face hearing his mother's voice telling him that Christmas was a family event and that he should be at home, not gallivanting around some foreign mountain. She never understood.

3

It's All Coming Together Nicely, But . . .

The journey from Tonbridge was uneventful. Peter liked his direct injection diesel. It was a very economical car, considering the power, and it liked the open road: a chance to blow through some of the accumulation of diesel soot, which built up in the exhaust with constant town use.

Arriving outside Sue's waterfront, Chiswick flat, nothing seemed to have changed. It was just as Peter remembered. Why had he left it so long? A silly question, really. He had arrived a few minutes too early and rather than appear over-eager, he sat and listened to the radio for ten minutes, just time to catch the news headlines at 8.00 p.m.: nothing special, just lots of talk about the run-up to Christmas and how much people were expecting to spend. *What a waste of money!* thought Peter.

He eventually got out of his silver-grey, metallic-finish diesel Skoda and rang the doorbell. A voice from the internal intercom said, 'Come on up; the door's open.'

Very trusting, thought Peter. *What if I'd been someone else?*

Sue was waiting at the top of the staircase. She looked radiant: not too much make-up, a simple blouse and knee-length, light blue skirt. Her hair was different, shorter, thought Peter.

'Hello, Peter, you made good time, then,' she remarked.

Peter owned up that he really arrived early but sat in the car listening to music.

'I know; I saw you through the curtains as I was getting ready. I appreciated the extra few minutes just to make sure everything was under control,' said Sue.

Peter took off his black, leather jacket and walked through into her lounge/diner. The curtains were drawn back and the view down the river was breath-taking, the riverside lights twinkling on the still waters.

Peter turned and faced Sue. 'It's really lovely to see you again, Sue. I hope you didn't mind too much me springing this on you, but there was no one else I wanted to discuss this with other than you.'

Sue looked at him. He had not changed that much; perhaps he looked slightly more mature facially. His hair was slightly longer but not untidy.

'I feel honoured, whatever it is you want to talk about. But before we get down to really serious matters, I've poured us each a Kir Royale. I seem to remember it's one of your favourite tipples.'

Peter sat on the sofa and Sue came and sat next to him, her skirt slightly riding up to reveal part of her thigh, which in turn told him she was not wearing tights. He must concentrate!

'Sue, it's about work.'

'You haven't got the sack, Peter,' she cut in.

'No, nothing like that. I've been offered an opportunity that's really too good to pass up and I need your advice,' said Peter, putting down his glass and waiting for her response.

Sue looked him squarely in the eye. He really was more handsome than she remembered. What a shame her job in London had kept them apart all this time. 'Well, if you've got promotion or been offered a good job elsewhere, why do you need to ask me? You always were your own man, Peter. You've done well so far; I've not really lost touch with all that you've achieved. I've even seen your byline on more than one occasion.'

Peter was quite taken aback. He had thought she didn't care; now she was telling him that she *had* been aware of what he had been up to. He wondered just how deeply this went. Was it just his work or had her interest strayed into his personal life as well?

'It's all happened so quickly, Sue. One minute I was beginning to make a name for myself on a good countywide weekly, the next moment the editor-in-chief from the group comes and tells me I can produce a whole series of travel features – including doing the travelling!'

'Oh, Peter. That's great news. You've always wanted to travel. Now is your big chance. Why the doubt? Why come to me when you really know the answer yourself?' said Sue, obviously showing delight for Peter's good news.

'Yes, I am pleased. It's too good a chance to pass up but . . . well, Sue, you are more a girl of the world these days. You get the chance to meet important people, celebrities. I know you've been to America a couple of times on photo shoots. I'm sure once I get into it, I can do a good job but I value your opinion, Sue. Do you think I'm doing the right thing?'

Peter picked up his glass and gulped down more of the Kir than he really intended to. Sue pretended not to notice. She looked at Peter for a few minutes then leaned over and kissed him on the cheek. 'You silly old soppy thing! Of course you're doing the right thing. Ever since college, you knew your own mind, set your sights on what you wanted, not on what other people thought was best for you. I'm flattered you thought you should ask me, but I know you, Peter Kingston. You have already made up your mind on this one. There is more to this visit than you're currently letting on!'

Peter thought about that remark. Sue had an uncanny knack of being able to read his thoughts. Now he started to blush, realising his ulterior motives had been rumbled.

'The boss thinks I should start with a series of articles about the growth in winter sports, so I've being doing some quick research down at our local travel agents. The manager seems to know his stuff and has been on a couple of fact-finding trips over the past couple of years. Says Europe is really the place to write about; USA has a bit of a glamour appeal but the numbers are still small and in any case, the resorts don't have the romantic appeal of some European alpine countries. Chocolate box villages nestling amongst the pine trees and ski slopes right outside the hotel front door.' Peter stopped for another sip of his Kir, this time remembering not to gulp it down.

'Christmas is coming up and I thought a couple of articles about the kids: snow-covered Christmas trees and all that rubbish. Get a few quotes from mums and dads on what it was like to take children away over the festive season. What do you think?' asked Peter, focusing hard on Sue's glowing features.

'Peter, I think that's a great start. It wouldn't matter whether you chose Switzerland or Austria; they have always been firm favourites with British skiers. Anyway, let's eat. Otherwise the food will be spoiled. We can continue discussions over the meal.'

Sue grabbed Peter's hand and led him to the dining table by the picture window, overlooking the Thames. 'Now, you pour the wine while I bring in the food. It's not much but it will keep the wolf from the door,' she said, disappearing off in the direction of the kitchen.

Peter sat gazing out of the window. It suddenly felt as if he and Sue had never been parted. Her enthusiasm was already giving him an appetite to get on with the series. Then she was back: smoked salmon decorated with king prawns and delicately cut slices of brown bread and butter.

'My, you have been busy, and to think I wanted to take you out for a meal,' said Peter happily, filling both their glasses with a chilled Muscadet.

Sue sat at the opposite end of the small table. Peter thought she looked positively glowing and might have been in danger of staring had Sue not suggested they start eating.

'I could say eat up before it gets cold but that would be silly,' she smiled.

Peter always enjoyed seafood. Sue had remembered. *Oh Sue! How silly I have been to have neglected you for so long*, thought Peter.

They were halfway through when Sue broke the silence. 'If you are going to start your series at Christmas, how much travel planning have you done, Peter? Flights might be heavily booked and what about a hotel, even a resort? Have you thought this through yet?'

Peter swallowed his last prawn and putting down his small, silver knife and fork, decided to wash it down with some more Muscadet before replying. 'Actually, I'm going by car. Now, before you start accusing me of being crazy, this part I have thought through and even discussed with the travel agent. Seems car travel to the Alps is the really 'cool' way of getting there, not just for families, but for groups of friends as well. Seems you can save an absolute bomb on the cost of the holiday. Tour operators will give you a discount of up to a hundred and twenty pounds per person if you travel by car and the deal includes the ferry from Dover to Calais. You can take more baggage by car, especially important with kids, and you can hire or buy a ski box quite reasonably, not only to transport skis and boots, but also to fit your extras in. So this leaves more room inside the car,' said Peter, now relishing his recently acquired knowledge of the business.

Sue rose from the table. 'I'd better get the main course before all this knowledge completely throws me, Peter. Shan't be a mo.' And with that, she collected up the two plates and briskly disappeared again to the kitchen.

Peter reflected on the conversation so far. Sue had generously welcomed his news and the concept of what he had planned, but the idea of driving, well, she appeared to have some reservations. He would continue on a different tack.

He opened the Merlot and Sue re-appeared with the main meal: cannelloni garnished with broccoli in butter with oven-fried, sliced potatoes. It looked lovely.

'Oh, Sue; you've gone to a lot of trouble,' said Peter.

Sue beamed. 'Not really, Peter, dear; I have to own up and say it all comes from the Sainsbury's supermarket just down the road. I popped in on the way home and just grabbed a few things. They only take a few minutes in the microwaves, you know.'

Peter helped himself to some more broccoli and potatoes. Sue passed over the bottle of Merlot, knowing it was one of Peter's favourites. They ate for a few minutes in silence, savouring the meal before Peter remarked, 'Sue, this is such a lovely flat with perfect views and you've done so well for yourself on the magazine, but do you really enjoy the work?'

Sue put down her knife and fork, filled up their two wine glasses and replied, 'Peter, it's been the best thing that could have happened to me workwise. I get to meet some very important people, go on some marvellous photo shoots and my copy doesn't get so hacked about these days. The editor even invites me to put ideas forward on possible picture features and our magazine sales are going up in leaps and bounds.'

Peter was impressed and said so. It was obvious that Sue was destined to remain in London and although Tonbridge was only an hour's drive away, they really existed in different worlds.

Sue read his thoughts. 'Peter, don't look so glum. This travel thing could lead to the opening you need. But don't try and run before you can walk. Journalism is a hazardous business – here today, gone tomorrow. Your career at Tonbridge has gone really well so far and it's obvious that head office have been keeping an eye on you. Do well at this series of travel features, as I'm sure you will, and, well, who knows? You might get talent spotted by one of the Sundays or even a top magazine.'

They finished the rest of their meal in silence, Peter reflecting on Sue's words. 'Sue, that was all lovely,' he finally said. 'I feel a right heel pressuring you into tonight, you going to all this trouble and I suppose my ulterior motive was I wanted to share my news with you, but, above all, I wanted to see you again.'

'Peter Kingston, you are a real sweetie and I love you dearly. Now let's stop all this nonsense. I've got some cheese and biscuits and coffee coming up, and then I want to discuss your travel plans some more. Friday's only a few days away and you've got to get that plan of action ready.'

Peter helped Sue out to the small but well-fitted kitchen with the dirty dishes. She told him the dishwasher would do all the work then said, 'Go and sit by the fire and I'll bring in the cheese and the coffee.'

Peter did as he was told. *What a wife she'll make somebody someday*, he thought to himself.

They nibbled on a little cheese and sipped their black coffee as they sat together on the dark green, leather sofa. Sue invited Peter to try some Napoleon brandy and then she asked if he had selected a resort for his Christmas story.

'I've quickly looked at brochures on Austria and Switzerland. Obviously it has to be a resort that's both ideal for Christmas and for families. The short answer is no, not a definite resort, but I'm leaning towards one in Austria.'

Sue, playing devil's advocate, asked Peter why he didn't think one in Switzerland would be better. 'After all, Peter, surely Switzerland's more traditional and attracts more British skiers.'

Peter said he had balanced up the pros and cons. 'Cow bells and chocolate-box type winter scenes, but then, well, cows are kept indoors throughout the long winter months and apart from a few resorts, such as Davos, St Moritz and Lenk, sleigh rides seem more prolific in Austria. Also, Austrian resorts, according to statistics, seem to provide a more traditional Christmas and attract British families in greater numbers than the Swiss,' said Peter, hurriedly adding the facts that had come from his travel agent.

Sue was prepared to accept this without further question. 'But your plan of action for the boss will have to have a start, middle and end, with good explanations as to the whys and wherefores. Tomorrow is Tuesday, so we only have a couple of days to get this thing drafted out,' she said.

Peter picked up on her words immediately. 'We!' he cried. 'What do you mean, "we"?'

Sue took his hand and pulled Peter closer to him. 'Peter, darling, you have come here asking for help. Well, I'd love to help so tomorrow you can draft something out, email it to me and I'll email something back in the way of comment by the end of the day. That will give you Wednesday and Thursday to really polish it up and by

Friday morning, you could be kissing your office goodbye for a few months. And that brings me to the next important point. After three glasses of wine, one of Kir and a substantial brandy, you can't possibly drive back to Tonbridge and it's already past eleven, so you'd better stay the night and travel back in the morning. You'll be heading against the rush hour, so you shouldn't have any bother in getting to the office in reasonable time. Now I've put out a towel and flannel in the bathroom, so you go first. Off you go and don't argue!'

Peter could have argued. But he didn't want to. Sue could be pretty firm when she wanted to be, but things were again moving faster than he had really expected.

Twenty minutes later, Sue came into the bedroom and looked at him. Peter wanted to say he hoped he was not being presumptuous, but no words were really necessary. Peter wore his boxer shorts; Sue wore a fetching and certainly revealing shorty nightie, which also revealed the outline of her fantastic breasts. The electric blanket had been on long enough to take the chill off the sheets, but Sue immediately cuddled up close to him.

'Oh, Peter, it's been such a long, long time and I've truly missed you, but I was not sure you cared anymore. Don't say anything, Peter darling. Let's pretend the months that have passed have really been days.'

Peter kissed her on her lips and she responded by putting her arms tightly round him and pulling him even closer. He felt her body immediately begin to respond but did not really want to rush anything.

'Sue.'

'Shhh, Peter! Don't say a word.'

So he didn't; he simply kissed her more, on her lips, her neck and her arms as she pulled off her nightie. Her breasts were as firm as he had remembered, her nipples hard and inviting. *Oh bliss. Can this be real or am I dreaming?* he thought as her body moved under his and they came together as naturally as a foot slides into a sock.

4

The Alps Beckon

They made love twice, the second time as the sun was rising across London and the Thames. Sue had already slipped out of bed and was getting ready in the bathroom. Peter lay on the bed covered only with a sheet. It had been a wonderful night, snuggling up to Sue had seemed so natural and relaxing, so much so Peter had put thoughts of his newspaper and travel to one side just to thoroughly absorb this beautiful young lady lying next to him. But now, in the cold light of day, one instinct was to continue to enjoy the moment, but on the other hand he really felt very excited about the future and he was ready to put pen to paper.

Sue re-appeared. 'I must be in the office before nine. I have to discuss yesterday's photo shoot with the editor and there may be questions about why I declined the client's dinner invitation last night.'

Peter smiled at her. 'Sue, it was really great; you don't realise just how your eagerness in this new project has inspired me. I will certainly get an email to you during the afternoon and perhaps we can speak on the phone this evening.'

Sue agreed it would be okay. 'Tuesday evening's housework night. A girl needs to keep on top of things occasionally,' she said, leaning over and giving him a kiss on the cheek. 'I've left some breakfast cereal and orange juice out for you. Just pull the door when you leave and, Peter, it really was good last night, wasn't it.' It was a statement that needed no answer. Both knew they had rekindled something that had really never gone away.

Peter showered, had some juice and a small bowl of cornflakes. He checked he had everything – not that he had come with much other than himself – and closed the flat door behind him. It was 8.15 a.m.; an hour's drive back to Tonbridge against the flow of rush hour traffic should be about right.

It was just after 9.30 a.m. when he parked the car and briskly walked up the stairs and into the newsroom. Dave immediately called him over.

'Nigel Ewell's case has been transferred to London's Horseferry Road Magistrates' Court and is scheduled for a further remand tomorrow. Just thought you might like to know. By the way, I liked your council story on the sewerage. I'm going to get young Andrew Forsythe to do a follow-up, talk to some of the residents about the mess and what amount of compensation they'll be seeking. I think, between the council officials and the contractors, there'll be some red faces for a few weeks yet.'

'Thanks for that,' said Peter. 'You know I've got to prepare a plan for John Riddell and have it on his desk first thing Friday morning, so I'll be getting on with a bit more research today if that's okay with you, Dave.'

Dave said it didn't present too many problems, but if a big story broke he would like Peter not too far away. 'If you have to go out, make sure I can get hold of you fairly quickly.'

'No problem,' said Peter.

He went over to his desk and got out the tour operators' brochures from the drawer. Christmas in Austria. He still had to tell his parents he was going away. Ah well, that was the least of his worries. He scanned the pages of all of those listing Austria. The Tirol seemed the most popular, but Peter knew there was more to Austria than just the Tirol. *This needs some imagination. No point in going for the obvious; it had better be some up and coming place attracting just enough British enthusiasts to make it interesting*, he thought to himself.

Eventually, Peter settled for a village called Altenmarkt, about forty-five minutes to an hour's drive south of Salzburg. The brochure said it formed part of a four-valley region with 114 lifts, 320 km of downhill skiing and was great for kids and the family. Known as Salzburgerland, it was reasonably new on the British market but had long been popular, not only with the Austrians themselves, but with Dutch and Belgian, as well as Swiss and the occasional Welsh ski enthusiast.

Peter rang the manager at the travel agents and asked his opinion.

'What a good choice, Peter. I went to that village last year and it's simply great. You wouldn't believe the vastness of the skiing area. The facilities for children are super; there are horse-drawn sleigh rides, indoor swimming, and Christmas is a real magical event. What's even more important is the journey time: only about eleven hours from Calais and motorway door-to-door.'

Peter was amazed. 'Are you seriously telling me I can drive to the other side of Salzburg from Calais in about eleven hours? I don't own a Ferrari, you know.'

'Give me until after lunch and I'll have a route map prepared for you. We have all routes across Europe on computer these days, thanks to a company called Autoroute. Personally, I don't agree with every route from start to finish but they are jolly good in providing the basic information,' he said.

Peter thanked him and said he would need to book accommodation in the village. 'I don't want anything too pretentious. I know I'm on expenses, but I'd better not go over the top,' he said.

The manager told Peter that things would have progressed by the time he came round after lunch.

Well, that's a start, thought Peter when the call was over. So Christmas in the depths of Austria, probably New Year as well. Where would he move on to after that? My, there was going to be a lot to do by Friday.

A cup of coffee arrived on his desk. He looked up; it was 10.30 a.m. already.

By lunchtime, Peter had mapped out an itinerary, which had got him through to March: kids in the snow over Christmas, early January would be an article on uncluttered slopes for those who could get away without the worry of taking kids out of school. That would be in the Tirol. He had estimated a drive of about two hours to what was described as the 'historic walled town of Kitzbühel, famous for the Men's downhill Hahnenkamm race'. *That should be fun*, thought Peter.

He popped over to the pub and Dorothy was in her usual cheerful mood. Peter ordered steak and kidney and half a shandy, and went to his usual corner table. Young Andrew Forsythe came in and headed over. *Oh no!* thought Peter. *I bet Bert Maynard wants me.*

Andrew sat down. 'Mind if I join you, Peter? Hear you're off to do some European travel stories. Lucky chap. Want anyone to carry your bags?'

Peter looked at young Andrew. He had a lot to learn but was eager and had quite a pleasant personality. 'You should be so lucky, Andrew. I think you're going to be busy enough while I'm away. I thought you were supposed to be following up my story about the sewerage and all the residents demanding compensation?'

Andrew said he was getting on with it that afternoon. 'Just thought I would have a spot of lunch first and see if you had any pointers for me. I want to make a good job of this one, not just because it was your original story, but it might do me some good in the long run. After my exams in June and providing I qualify, I'd like to stay on the paper and work my way up. I reckon there'll be some changes in the coming months and I'd like to be well placed.'

Peter remembered when he had been a 'cub reporter'. It seemed an age ago. But it wasn't really. Yes, he liked Andrew and would help him if he could. He remembered the help he had been given by his mentor, Tony: an absolutely brilliant reporter who should have been tops in Fleet Street, but had liked county regional weeklies, so he had spent his life 'out in the sticks' and made a name for himself on a rival paper, now sadly merged with his own. Tony had taken early retirement two years ago, but still did quite a bit of linage for various news outlets.

Peter took a sip of his shandy, then said, 'You could always go for the hardship angle. Christmas is coming up; see if any Christmas toys have been damaged or ruined by the sewerage; see who'll be having a miserable Christmas because of the stench in their home; see who was insured and perhaps find someone who wasn't; find an elderly pensioner, perhaps living alone who has nobody to turn to. There are plenty of angles.'

Andrew was thrilled. 'That's great, Peter. I hope I can be as good as you one day. Wow! There's enough here to get my teeth into.'

Peter's food arrived and they sat in silence for the next ten minutes. Peter's final piece of advice to Andrew was to watch his back. 'Neither the council nor the contractors are going to like this one. They may start putting obstacles in your way. If in doubt, speak to Bert Maynard. Get him on your side. He likes being asked for advice. Don't play the know-all and then find you're doing a rewrite.'

They chatted for a few more minutes before Peter made his excuses. Time was marching on and he had to get round to the travel agents. The manager, good to his word, presented him with a computer printout of the route from Calais.

'I've managed to get you a room in that little hotel in Altenmarkt. I'd say you were jolly lucky to get accommodation this late, but it helped that I had been there and they remembered me. I told them you were a journalist doing an article on their village. The owner is on the local council and he'll speak with the tourist office direct, get you fixed up with whatever you want. You'll find everyone and everything is open over the whole Christmas period. It's their bread and butter business, so to speak.'

Peter was impressed. He had not realised a local travel agent could be so helpful. 'Look, I've got to get my whole itinerary for the next few months approved by my editor-in-chief yet. Don't suppose there'll be any problems, though. Now, how do I get across the Channel? Can you arrange that for me as well?'

The manager assured him he could, but said Peter might like to contact the ferry company direct.

'I think they do something special for journalists. Worth trying. And you know better than me when you want to travel. I would suggest you have a word with them about insurance as well. I can sell you some, but they might have an inclusive ticket/insurance deal. By the way, you had better have some snow chains, just in case. It's compulsory throughout alpine regions in the winter.'

Peter asked if he had any suggestions. 'The best is a company down in Whitstable. Here's their number. They're really helpful, fixed me up last year and chains these days are really simple to fit.'

Peter's list was growing by the minute. What a lot to think about, what a lot to do and this was only the beginning of his travels.

Back at the office, Peter emailed an outline of his ideas to Sue. *Wonder what she'll make of it really*, he thought. Next, he rang the ferry company and got through to the press office. Yes, they would be pleased to help, especially if he were mentioning them in his article. The chap told Peter there was a ferry roughly every forty minutes, day and night, and a booking would not really be a problem. They could even fix him up with travel and winter sports insurance, but they would want to know by Friday lunchtime at the latest. Peter promised to get back to them by then.

Next, he rang the snow chain company and said he could call over Friday after lunch. He gave them the make and model of his car. No, he did not have the tyre size but they thought it would be the standard wheel size.

Clothes! *Oh blast, I had better get that sorted.* He would go down to the local C&A and see what they had.

It was mid-afternoon when Peter returned, smiling at his success. He had got everything he should need in the way of winter clothing: anorak, salopettes, thermals, gloves, socks and quite a nice woolly hat. Next, he had to ring his mother.

'Mum, I'll be round for dinner this evening. I've got something important to tell you and dad . . . Can't speak now . . . See you about seven,' and he put down the phone. This evening was not going to be enjoyable.

He was just going through some papers in his drawer when the phone rang. It was Sue.

'Peter, it all looks good to me. I think you should expand on the theme of each piece, though: kids away in the snow at Christmas; New Year in the Alps; the quietness of January; doing the downhill racing circuit, etc. etc. I should think your boss is going to expect a little meat on the bone at this stage,' said Sue.

Peter was really warming to the whole thing now. But there were a thousand and one things still to do. For a start, he had better warn Melissa that he was going away for a while. That would not be quite as difficult as telling his parents that evening, but she tended to be a bit clingy and would want to go with him. *Fat chance!* thought Peter.

He arrived home just before 7.00 p.m. His mother gave him the usual hug and kiss on the cheek. To her, her little boy was still just that. His father was in the lounge, drawing on his pipe and catching up on some reading.

'Hello, Peter. Hear you've got some news for us. Hope it's advancement on the paper. You deserve it, you know.'

Peter poured himself and his mother a sherry.

'Dinner will be about fifteen minutes yet. Come on then, Peter. Tell us the news,' said his mother.

'It's all a bit difficult, really,' said Peter, not sure whether to begin with the good or bad news.

'Come on, lad, spit it out. Must be good news, surely,' said his father, putting down his pipe and paper at the same time.

'Yes, well, it is good news. You see, the editor-in-chief has asked me to produce a whole series of travel articles. It's something new and they'll syndicate the articles through the whole group, probably even the daily on a Friday.'

'That's really great, my boy,' beamed his father. 'Always knew you were going places. What are you going to be writing about and when does it start?'

Peter looked down at his sherry, decided to take a gulp, looked up at his mother and said. 'Well, that's just it. I shall be making a start next week, getting something sent back over Christmas.'

'*Over Christmas*! What do you mean, Peter? Something *sent back*. You can't be going anywhere; you're having Christmas here!'

'Look Mother, I'm a grown man and ambitious as a journalist. This is not the time to let sentimental family gatherings get in the way of a once-in-a-lifetime chance to do something I have always wanted to do. I am sorry, Mother, but I have made up my mind. You will have to face this Christmas without me!'

His parents looked at each other. It was his father who spoke first.

'I say, Peter old chap, this is all a bit short notice and unreasonable on your mother. I know I have always pressured you to get on and do well, but being away at Christmas? Shall I speak to your editor in the morning?'

'You will do no such thing, Father. I am old enough to make my own decisions now. This is too good an opportunity to be passed up and I don't expect any interference,' said Peter, sounding a little too harsh.

His mother jumped up from her chair and ran to the kitchen in tears.

'Now look what you have done, Peter. Damned unfair on your mother I would say,' and with that, his father picked up his whisky and followed his wife to the kitchen.

Oh, lummy! thought Peter. This is going to be one of those evenings. A silent meal and a real atmosphere!

His parents returned to the table after a short period and the meal resumed in silence. It wasn't until Peter had finished pudding, his favourite of treacle sponge and custard, that his father spoke.

'I have convinced your mother that work is work and you probably had no choice in the matter. We might not view your absence as something to be looked forward to, but if you have decided that work comes first, then so be it.'

Peter looked at them both. 'Well, at least I'll be around until Sunday and anyway, I'll telephone you Christmas morning. Just think of the numerous families in the same boat where a son or daughter, not out of choice, is going to be away. Don't take this the wrong way, Mother, but I simply cannot be tied to your apron strings forever. I'm in my twenties now and must get on with my life. Sure, I would like to have been at home over Christmas but this opportunity is too good to pass up, really.'

With that, he got up and took the dirty dishes to the kitchen. As he left the room, he could hear his parents having a heated argument. *Oh well, what's done is done*, he thought and when he returned, he made an excuse about getting some papers together and went to his room. He would telephone Melissa tomorrow. He had had quite enough arguments this evening for one day.

The following two days were spent putting the final touches to his ideas to be presented to his editor-in-chief on Friday morning. Peter was just about to print off the final version mid-afternoon on Thursday when the telephone on his desk rang.

It was Sue.

'Peter, I have had the most wonderful of ideas. How about me coming with you over Christmas and New Year to do some pictures? My magazine say they would lap up a photo feature of British kids having a real white Christmas and perhaps your own travel feature should be illustrated with something other than the run of the mill, tourist office library shots.'

Peter was stunned into silence.

'Hello! Are you there, Peter? Say something!'

It took Peter a little time for the idea to sink in. *Sue with me over Christmas and New Year? What a great idea, but then, what will the boss say?* 'You've knocked me flat with this one, Sue. It sounds really great. Are you sure your editor supports this or is it all your own idea?'

Sue sounded offended. 'Peter Kingston, you sound as if you don't really want me along. You haven't got someone else lined up for this, have you?'

Peter thought he had better repair some fences quickly. 'Don't be silly, Sue. It's a really wonderful idea and I hadn't even thought about taking *anyone* with me. But if I were going to take someone, it could only be you.'

Peter told Sue that he was just printing off the travel schedule ideas ready for the morning's meeting. 'I can't see the boss is going to have any objections; hopefully he'll like the idea of pictures to accompany my first feature. But I'd better offer to pay all of your expenses. The costs should not be too great – after all, the fuel for the car, ferry crossing, insurance and other journey costs will be paid for by my paper. There will obviously be your extra meals and also your return air fare home, but maybe your magazine will be prepared to meet some of your expenses if you produce photos for them as well. Have you thought this through, Sue? What about special clothes?' asked Peter.

Sue assured him nothing would be a problem. 'Just get everything cleared in the morning, give me a call and I've got the rest of the day to get things sorted. I'll even get my magazine to arrange my travel insurance. But you'd better make sure the ferry ticket is for two people and that there's a bed for me at the hotel. I don't want to be sleeping on the floor on Christmas Eve.'

Peter heard her chuckle down the phone.

'No problems. Look, I'll call you tomorrow mid-morning and let you know how things have gone at head office.'

Peter knew his next mission was to sweet talk Melissa. So he phoned and asked if it was okay to pop round to her flat at about 7.00 p.m. 'Perhaps we could go out for a meal,' he suggested.

Melissa said that would be nice, so, clearing everything with Dave Edwards, he left early to get ready.

When he arrived at Melissa's flat, he received the usual warm embrace.

'Are you staying tonight, Peter? I'll get things ready before we go out.'

Peter held her at arm's length as he answered. 'I'm not sure. Look, let's go and enjoy a nice Chinese meal. I've got some news for you about my work, which is going to change things for a while. We can talk things over during the meal.'

Melissa showed a worried frown but she knew Peter better than to push him into a corner.

'Okay, I'm ever so hungry and Christmas is only a few days away now. I'm planning to get most of my shopping and last-minute presents this weekend.'

Peter sighed. This evening was going to be difficult.

They walked to the restaurant. It was about twenty minutes away and she told Peter that council staff were getting ten days off. 'Some of it is like forced holidays on staff to save the council money. They don't want to re-open until after New Year, so we've all had to save a few days of our holiday entitlement to accommodate them.'

The restaurant was only half full and they had no trouble getting a table. Peter and Melissa had often eaten there before and the staff recognised them.

Peter ordered a lager to start with and a pot of Chinese tea with the meal. Melissa said she would have the same and they ordered a set meal for two. Their tastes were very similar.

After the lager arrived, Melissa said, 'Well, Peter, tell me the news about your work. What's happening?'

Peter outlined everything that had happened, conveniently leaving out any reference to Sue. 'So you see, tomorrow morning will tell whether my ideas find favour at head office.'

Melissa looked very angry. 'Peter, are you seriously telling me you have brought me out to dinner just to say you're going away Sunday and I won't be seeing you for at least two months? And I was so looking forward to us spending time at Christmas together!'

The chicken soup arrived and Peter said they ought to start. Between spoonfuls, he repeated what he had told his parents: the opportunity was too good to pass up, that it was nothing to do with her and the time would go quickly.

Melissa put down her spoon and exclaimed, 'I'll come with you. I've got all this spare time off over Christmas and at least we'll be together.'

Peter gulped down the next spoonful. This was going to be more difficult than he had thought.

'Melissa, look, as much as the idea appeals, it's just not practical. I shall be working hard all of the time and travelling all around, fixing up the next stage of my itinerary and besides, how would you get home?'

'Fly,' said Melissa, getting really excited.

Peter decided it was time to put his foot down firmly. 'No, Melissa, it's simply out of the question. I must do this alone without any distractions. I'll send you some postcards and anyway, you can see how things are going by reading my articles when they go to print.'

Melissa was not convinced and was obviously still angry. She told him so and Peter was no longer enjoying his Chinese meal. Several times, he tried to change the subject, but Melissa kept on about how lovely it would be to go with him. It got to the point where Peter decided to ask for the bill and say it was time to go home.

'I've got an early start tomorrow. Must be one hundred per cent for the boss at head office,' he said with determination.

Melissa reluctantly put on her coat and they walked back to her flat in silence. They went inside and Melissa made Peter a coffee.

'At least please stay tonight, Peter. I won't be too demanding. I know you have to be alert in the morning!'

Peter considered the offer. It might be his last chance for at least two months, if not forever. 'Okay, but I have to telephone home. Things are pretty fraught there.'

When he made the call, his mother answered and Peter said he would be home the next day. 'I'll tell you how the meeting went, Mother,' he added and with that, he quickly put down the phone.

Later that night, even Melissa's energetic lovemaking did little to arouse Peter into his usual passionate self. Melissa sensed something was wrong but didn't want to cause even more friction. She knew her love for Peter was deeper than anything he was likely to give in return, but she found the warmth of his body somehow comforting, even if he were going to be away for ages. He had been her first and only love and she had decided there was no one else she wanted, ever!

The following morning, Peter was up and showering at 6.30 a.m. He wanted to be at his best and always kept spare clothes at Melissa's. It had become like a second home. He wore a light blue shirt, burgundy-red tie and a plain, charcoal-grey suit with black shoes. It wasn't as though Peter didn't usually look smart; he just wanted to create a good impression.

'Oh, you do look really smart,' said Melissa. 'Give me a ring at work when you have some news and, Peter, I'm really sorry about last night. Of course your work comes first and I should be encouraging you, not giving you a hard time. Will you forgive me?'

Peter felt a right heel. He knew he should tell Melissa that Sue was back on the scene, but he didn't want to burn all his bridges. The Sue relationship might not come to anything and some might say he was hedging his bets.

Peter promised to ring, walked to the office, collected his car and drove through the Friday morning, rush hour traffic to head office, arriving with at least twenty minutes to spare. The editor-in-chief's secretary, Elisabeth, was already at her desk.

'Hello, Peter. Heard you were coming. He's in but got someone with him. I'm sure he won't be long,' she said, smiling.

Peter took his proposal from his briefcase and read through the itinerary and ideas for the series of travel features. He felt reasonably pleased that he had covered most points. He was just getting to the end when the door opened and a familiar face appeared. It was Chris Hodges, one of the crime reporters who reported on most of the crime stories from the region for the evening paper and covered all the important court cases involving the bigger crime stories.

'Hi, Peter. How are things? Hear on the grapevine you're off to do a bit of globetrotting. Lucky fellow. I'm following up on this Nigel Ewell case now that it's been transferred to London. I think the hit and run involving poor old Bob Hoskins was terrible. He's likely to be in hospital for a couple of months yet, but at least he's making some progress. The head injuries are not as bad as first feared.'

Elisabeth (she hated being called Liz) came over and interrupted their conversation. 'Sorry to butt in, but he's ready for you now, Peter.'

'Thanks, Elisabeth. Well, Chris, great seeing you again. All the best with the Ewell case; it should produce some good copy. I'll send you a postcard,' he said, smiling, and went into his editor-in-chief's office.

When the handshakes were over, Peter sat down in the oak-panelled room, wall-to-wall carpeted with two leather armchairs either side of the window and produced the sheets of paper. 'I've prepared an itinerary plus ten ideas for various travel features, all based on holidays in the Alps. Starting with kids enjoying a white Christmas, I've included one on how adults without children to worry about can go out of season and get some great reductions as well as enjoy uncrowded slopes. Then I thought of one about the various ways of getting to the various alpine regions. Health seems to be important, so I thought a feature on a health spa where you can swim in a heated pool outdoors surrounded by snow, breathe in sulphur to clear the airwaves and go for long walks through snow-covered valleys. I've even researched a resort where one minute you can do the Cresta Run and the next minute learn how to drive on snow and ice on a special circuit.'

John Riddell, a youthful, clean-shaven looking man not displaying his 51 years and wearing a sports jacket, tie and black trousers, smiled and said, 'Peter, it seems to me my views on your capabilities were not unfounded. I'm really impressed. Yes, all is sanctioned and my secretary has got a few things to give you. I shall want the first feature faxed here by Saturday. I'm planning to run it on the Monday following. Think you can manage that?'

Peter assured John Riddell he could. He then broached the subject of Sue. 'I had an idea about pictures; thought we could illustrate the articles by finding a few families from our own region. I have a friend who is a photographer and can come along at no cost to us, of course, and we can wire back some pictures. Would that be okay?'

'It seems an excellent idea to me. Of course we would pay for the pictures, always providing that young lady of yours uses something different for her own magazine.'

Peter was dumbfounded.

'Peter Kingston, there is not much escapes me. I'm not prying into your private life and go with my blessing. Just remember, this is an important work assignment, not a free holiday for you and the love of your life. Keep things in perspective,' John Riddell said, smiling.

Peter put the sheets of paper on the desk and thanked the editor-in-chief for his confidence. 'I won't let you down, sir. I have really set my heart on doing a good job.'

'I know you won't, otherwise you wouldn't be going. Keep me posted with progress and draw some expenses. I've already warned the accountant you will want funds and a facility to draw down to cover the two months. By the way, you had better give Elisabeth the name of your first hotel and a phone number. We will certainly wish to keep in touch.'

Peter left the office. It was 9.45 a.m. Had he really been in there forty-five minutes? My, how time flies.

'Wish I was coming with you, Peter,' Elisabeth told him as he passed her desk. 'I think you'll be the envy of every newsroom throughout the group. I've got an envelope with some bits and pieces that he asked me to give you: insurance cover from the paper, my own fax number so everything should come here, plus an Internet web site number so that all your stuff can be backed up on that to make life easier. And if you have any problems, my direct phone line as well. When are you off?'

'Sunday ferry from Dover. Our local travel agent's been really helpful and I've got to ring the ferry company to confirm the travel arrangements. They said they look after travel journalists, so new doors are opening,' said Peter, beaming, before giving her the name of the hotel and phone number.

Elisabeth got up, handed him the envelope and leaned over to give him a kiss. 'That's on account. You can return the favour when you come back. I hear winter sunshine in the Alps gives a person a real good suntan. Have fun, Peter.'

With that, he left the office feeling very pleased with himself. He drove back to his own office then knocked at Bert Maynard's door and walked in.

'Hello, Peter. I've had a phone call from head office and I hear you did a really good presentation job. No surprise really. I'll miss your writing style and nose for a good story, but I've been promised another senior from elsewhere in the group while you're away and young Forsythe really fancies his chances at the big time. I'll have to rein him in a bit until we see the results of his exams in June. But he's willing, and he looks up to you. Did you know that? He tells me you gave him some good pointers for the sewerage article.'

Peter was slightly embarrassed. 'I'll miss the office and all of you. I have tried to give young Andrew some pointers as if I was handling the story myself, but the rest is now down to him. How on earth could I have foreseen such an opportunity? And if I get a sniff of another story that might be of interest, I'll send it through.'

'You bet, Peter. You always had a gift for ferreting out a good story, so news or travel, it makes little difference here,' said his editor then shook him warmly by the hand. 'This is by no means farewell, just a slight interval in your career with us. Have fun, work hard and I'm sure you will impress the powers that be at head office. Don't forget where we are if you need anything . . . anything at all, Peter.'

Peter left his editor's office with a slight lump in his throat. It was like starting out on a huge adventure, but things were still moving so fast. He still had so much to organise, but then Dave stopped him before he could even make it back to his desk.

'Hi, Peter. Ready for the off or shall I find something for you to do this afternoon?' he said with a chuckle.

'Think I might pass on that one, Dave, if you don't mind. But keep my chair warm and my desk clear. I'll be back.'

'From my point of view, that cannot be soon enough, Peter. But enjoy yourself and I'll be eagerly awaiting your weekly features.'

Peter went over to his desk and first rang Sue. 'It's all agreed and he knows you are coming to do some pictures. I'll ring you tonight to make final arrangements. Is that okay?'

Sue said it was, so Peter then telephoned Melissa.

'Yes, I'll pop round this evening, Melissa, but I can't stay. So many last-minute things to do, but this morning really went well. My editor-in-chief has given me his full blessing but told me to concentrate and work hard, so that is what I am planning to do.'

Melissa was not impressed and tried to convince Peter that all work and no play was not a good thing. Peter held the phone slightly away from his ear as Melissa went on and on about still wanting to join him to provide some home comforts. Peter finally decided enough was enough and told her firmly. 'Melissa, my mind is made up. I'm sorry but no.'

Peter hung up and decided it was time to make a clean break. With his laptop under his arm, he waved his farewells to everyone else in the office.

'Take care!' called Dave. And with that, Peter was through the door and heading to the car park.

When he got home, his mother was busy in the kitchen. 'Do we see anything of you before you leave?' she enquired rather icily of her son.

'Look, Mum, don't be so silly. I'll spend the next two nights here, although it's an early departure Sunday morning. By the way, do you remember Sue? You know, from college? She went to that fashion magazine in London.'

'Oh, I remember, Peter. Very nice girl. Have you heard from her?'

'Better than that, Mother. Sue's coming with me to help with photographs for the first feature. It's all agreed by my editor and I hope it's okay, but she's staying here Saturday night.' And with that, he turned on his heels and went to his room, smiling.

Peter had a list of a thousand and one things to do. First, he rang the press office at the ferry company and confirmed he wanted to travel Sunday morning and there would be two. They agreed on the

8.15 a.m. departure from Dover to Calais. He was reminded that central European time was one hour ahead of UK time.

'So the ship docks at ten thirty,' said the press officer lady, who also told him that the tickets would be waiting for collection in the travel centre at Dover.

Next, he arranged to collect the snow chains and made a final call to the travel agent. Fortunately, the manager was there and confirmed the hotel room was a double.

'Not too much of a call for single rooms these days,' he told Peter.

After a quick spot of lunch, Peter headed off to his local garage, where they fitted headlamp beam converters, checked his oil, antifreeze, made sure that the windscreen washer bottle had sufficient anti-freeze strength and gave him a useful book on his vehicle contact addresses throughout Europe. Not that he thought he would need assistance; his diesel car had always been most reliable.

That evening, before popping round to Melissa's, Peter rang Sue and they agreed she would be at his house in Tonbridge by around 5.00 p.m. 'Mother knows you're coming. I left her a little in the dark about how we had been in touch again. But don't worry; you were always her favourite,' said Peter.

The parting from Melissa at her home was not easy, and Peter hadn't expected it to be: tears ran down Melissa's cheeks and she pleaded to be telephoned. He told her he would phone and send postcards, and tried to assure her. 'The time will pass quickly; you'll probably quickly forget me and find a new love of your life,' he said jokingly.

Melissa did not find the joke amusing. 'Peter Kingston, how could you say such a thing? You will always be the only person in my life.'

Whoops! thought Peter.

He spent most of Saturday finishing packing. He hoped the various hotels in which he would finish up had some sort of laundry service; how could he possibly take enough for three months plus all the winter clothing?

Sue arrived and received a warm greeting from Peter's parents. There were the obvious questions, which Sue patiently attempted to answer.

'I mentioned it to my editor who thought a feature for our magazine would be an excellent idea. Peter's editor wanted pictures for his feature, so there we are. A happy coincidence and a coming together of working minds, so to speak.'

Sunday morning, they were up at 5.00 a.m. and out of the house by 5.45 a.m. They had to check in at Dover by 7.45 a.m. at the latest, but being a Sunday morning, there was little or no traffic once they hit the M20 down to the port. Peter easily collected his tickets; in fact all of the formalities were easy. Everything was computerised, with no sign of passport or customs people. *What a difference to a few years ago when I last came through here*, thought Peter. And it just kept getting better, as they were given priority boarding. Journalists, it seemed, had some pulling power and once on board they were shown to club class, which was equivalent to a first-class lounge.

The steward said they were entitled to free champagne, but Peter and Sue said coffee and some biscuits would be adequate. When the tray arrived, however, two small bottles of champagne were on it.

'Might as well take them with you, celebrate on Christmas Day! Going skiing are we?' enquired the steward.

Peter, not wishing to give too much away, grunted a sort of reply and they were left in peace. There was then an announcement from the captain that the vessel was secured for sea and would be leaving the berth in a few minutes.

Well, here we go, thought Peter. *The start of the big adventure!*

If only he had known how true those thoughts would turn out to be.

5

Snow, Snow and More Snow!

It was a calm crossing and a typical winter's morning. The sun rose above the horizon as the ferry made its way across the Channel. They could see the coast of France long before they docked, but the crossing seemed so quick: about one hour from harbour to harbour.

Peter's car was the first off and they were soon out of the port, again with no sign of border formalities, and immediately onto a dual carriageway. As he drove, he couldn't help but notice the change in Calais – Overhead roads and flashing direction arrows. Peter had studied the route but he had been careful to give Sue the route map before they drove off the ship. 'Just in case I go wrong,' he said.

They headed up the coast on a new motorway towards Dunkirk and then branched off onto another motorway towards Lille. They crossed over into Belgium, again without any formalities. Peter, turning to Sue, remarked, 'This EU thing has made travel so easy. It's just like back home, driving from one county to another. No reason to stop!'

The Belgian town of Mons sped by. The legal speed was 120 kph, around 75 mph, and they were burning up the miles. At Namur, Peter had decided to head south across the Ardennes and into Luxembourg. This was a deviation from the recommended route but the travel agent said it was better, faster and quieter. He was right. The city of Luxembourg loomed up off to the left but the modern motorway skirted the European capital. Peter checked his watch.

Just three and a half hours after leaving Calais, they were well into Europe.

He had been told to follow a route to the border town of Remich, still just inside Luxembourg. It was apparently very picturesque and sat on the banks of the famous Moselle River. Germany was on the other side. Luxembourg's fuel was cheap and wine and spirits were at giveaway prices, or so Peter had been told.

They stopped at a petrol station and were impressed to find it had a supermarket selling just about everything. Doing a quick price conversion, Peter found his fuel would cost him approximately half of what he paid back home. Good quality wine was no more than £2.00 and a bottle of whisky was just over £5.00. The garage was offering customers free cups of coffee and a croissant.

Peter commented to Sue that it would be quite a good place to live. 'No wonder we're the poor relations of the rest of Europe at these sorts of prices,' he said.

They stretched their legs and set off again. It was 2.45 p.m. and they had decided to stop by 6 p.m. Peter told Sue as they headed into Germany that they should be heading towards Karlsruhe by that time.

They skirted Saarbrucken on yet another fine autobahn, passing the huge Ford car works at Saar Louis. They joined another motorway, indicating Karlsruhe was a further 185 km. *At around 80 mph, that would be about right*, thought Peter.

It was just before 6.00 p.m. when they stopped on the outskirts of the city on the banks of the River Rhine. They had spotted a small, but, nevertheless, friendly-looking German hotel. They booked a double room and were told they could have a meal in the restaurant any time up to 9.30 p.m. They decided an early meal, a stroll along the banks of the Rhine, followed by an early night, would be perfect.

They awoke to the sound of traffic, a lot of traffic, then remembered it was Monday morning.

'The rush hour starts as early here as it does back home,' said

Snow, Snow and More Snow!

Peter, looking over to Sue, who was obviously not sure she wanted to get up just yet.

'Peter, there's no rush is there? Just another half an hour, a leisurely breakfast and by the time we're ready to set out, most of the rush hour will be over. People start work by 8.00 a.m. out here.'

Peter decided another half an hour would be perfect. Sue looked perfect, her see-through nightie showing off her body to its best advantage. *Life is bliss,* thought Peter. It wouldn't have been as good had Sue not suggested she come along as well.

They showered and packed their bags. Breakfast was more than satisfying: cereal, a selection of cooked meats and cheese, and lots of welcoming coffee. When they were ready to leave, they paid the equivalent of £50.00 for the two of them.

'That's very reasonable, Sue. An evening meal, comfortable B&B. Where do we go wrong back in the UK?' It was a question that needed no answer. Rip-off Britain. Very true.

They had looked at the map over breakfast. Their route would take them from Karlsruhe to Stuttgart, Ulm and then Munich. The hotel owner explained it was a drive of nearly three hours but depended on the traffic. The road was good but Monday morning there were always 'vele Lastwagen,' said the hotel lady.

She was right. There were so many lorries. 'Do you realise that all this freight once upon a time would have gone by rail. Roads are so good that it's quicker and cheaper to load at the factory and unload at the customer's door. Saves intermediate handling,' said Peter.

They ran into their first snow shortly after passing Stuttgart Airport. The autobahn climbed and climbed over the hills. The temperature gauge on Peter's car showed that outside, the temperature was only just above freezing, but the roads were still clear, although the amount of snow gathering by the roadside was increasing.

They could see the tall buildings of Ulm from the motorway. The autobahn was really good and the miles sped by. Munich was now half an hour away and there was less heavy freight traffic.

Peter had been told there was a new motorway around the capital town of Bavaria, but he told Sue that it might be an idea for them to drive through, just to get a feel for the place. 'Besides, we need fuel and it's bound to be cheaper in the city than on the motorway. Do you know this part of Bavaria is at least five hundred metres above sea level?'

Sue didn't, but wasn't surprised. *Does it always snow here in winter*, she thought?

Signposting was really good. The main places, such as Garmisch, Innsbruck and Salzburg, were clearly shown. They stopped at an Aral Garage and filled up. It was also a comfort stop after all that coffee at breakfast time. Peter and Sue decided against any more food but they bought some fruit from a little shop next door to the garage.

The architecture of Munich was quite varied. There were rows and rows of flats, huge blocks of flats, but all painted in different colours, making them a little more attractive than plain stonework.

'Very few Germans own their own homes. I'm told land is hugely expensive so they prefer to live in flats in the city,' said Peter.

They passed the turn off for Garmisch and followed the direction for Innsbruck and Salzburg. Soon, they had left the Bavarian city behind and were once again on a fine autobahn. There were more cars now and more and more snow.

'I hope we can get into Austria before the roads become too difficult,' said Sue. 'The snow looks pretty on the fir trees, but I'm a bit worried about how fast everyone seems to be driving with this snow around. They must all be going skiing. Look at those special boxes on the roofs of the cars.'

Peter told her not to worry. The road wasn't actually that bad. 'I must just remember not to do any sudden braking. Don't worry, Sue, I'll keep my distance and my speed down.'

They estimated that Salzburg was only just over an hour's driving time beyond Munich and both commented that Europe must have been shrinking. To think that two famous cities in two different countries were only about 120 km apart.

Sue, looking at the map, said the mountains on the right must be shared between Germany and Austria. 'The border seems to run right along the top of the mountains,' she commented.

Peter had heard about Bavaria and even read somewhere that people skied in the Bavarian Alps. Glancing over at Sue, he said, 'If I hadn't seen the Bavarian Mountains, I wouldn't have guessed they were so high or covered in so much snow.'

By this time, the amount of snow on the road was getting deeper and Peter worried about road handling. 'If it gets much worse, I think I'll pull over at the next lay-by,' he said.

At that moment, in the distance, they couldn't believe what they were seeing. All the traffic had slowed down and one after another, three huge snow ploughs, painted in bright orange and followed by a green and white police car, came out of the lay-by. The cars were bunched up and hardly moving. In front, the three snow ploughs had positioned themselves, one in each lane and angled so the one in the outside lane was slightly ahead. They quickly set off, followed by the police car, which had positioned itself in the centre lane with blue lights flashing, and snow sprayed nicely to the nearside verge.

'That is what I call impressive snow clearing. Shame we're not close enough for you to get a photo, Sue. If people back home saw that, they'd think they were on another planet.'

Sue said to Peter, 'I do not think the UK even has three snow ploughs, let alone three to be spared for the same stretch of motorway at the same time,' with a wry smile.

'Don't be too cynical, Sue. After all, they have to be prepared for the worst of winter's conditions out here. But I know what you're saying. Half an inch of snow in Britain and the country grinds to a halt.'

They were surprised that the traffic was now moving at nearly 50 mph. The road surface was practically clear of snow and covered by a layer of sand. 'We shouldn't have any problems getting to the ski village if it's like this for the rest of the journey.'

After they had driven a little further, they saw a sign for Berchtesgaden.

'That's where Hitler had his mountain retreat during the Second World War,' commented Peter.

Sue, not wishing to sound too well educated as far as history went, simply grunted an acknowledgement.

They passed a huge, frozen lake and Sue, looking at the map, informed Peter that it was called Chiemsee. Then a border-crossing sign loomed up.

'Only eight kilometres to Austria. That travel agent was quite right; Austria is an easy drive really,' said Peter.

They continued their drive and as they neared Austria, they saw their first customs officer of the journey, who waved them down.

'I wonder what this is all about,' said Sue.

Peter wound down the window. The border policeman saluted, smiled and in quite good English, asked where they were heading to. Peter said they were spending Christmas and New Year in a small village called Altenmarkt.

'A good choice. You will like the skiing. It is near my own home town of Bischofshofen. But to reach it you travel on one of our fine autobahns and here in Austria, you need to purchase a special tax disc. Otherwise, you must keep to the – how do you say? – small streets, and in winter that is not so good, ja!'

Peter was directed to park his car and go to a small office marked *Vignette*. 'You will not find it expensive,' said the policeman. 'I wish you a wonderful stay in Austria.'

Peter thanked him and Sue decided to stretch her legs. 'This is a novel experience. Perhaps we should charge visitors to use our motorways,' she said.

'I don't think ours are worth paying for. They usually start and finish in the wrong place and create huge bottlenecks where they finish,' said Peter.

The official in the office asked how long they would be staying and informed them that they could have a vignette for ten days, two months or a whole year.

'One for two months,' said Peter, remembering that he was not here for a Christmas holiday but would be travelling from one area to the next. At £7.50, it seemed ridiculously cheap.

'Do you know, Sue, on French motorways, you pay at every péage for every journey. I'm told a journey from Calais to the South of France can cost over forty pounds – and that's one way! And we talk about rip-off Britain!'

They walked back to the car. The weather was getting a lot worse. Snow was falling thick and hard. The temperature gauge showed it was -3 degrees outside.

'We don't get snowflakes this large at home,' said Sue. 'Are we going to be alright without chains?'

Peter said they would drive slowly and see how things went. It was getting dark but their final destination shouldn't be far. 'I'm sure the Austrians are equal to the Germans when it comes to keeping main routes open. After all, the Christmas car traffic needs to be kept down. It's their bread and butter business after all,' said Peter, remembering a phrase used by his travel agent.

Beyond the border crossing, the autobahn divided: Salzburg City and Linz to the left. 'We need to branch off right towards a place called Villach,' Sue told Peter.

As he slowly drove on, traffic was still heavy and nearly everyone was passing them.

'I'd rather continue at this slow speed, just in case,' he told Sue, and then mountains loomed ahead of them out of the darkness.

'Surely we're not going over those!' said Sue.

Far from it; they went beneath them. The autobahn disappeared into a brightly lit tunnel and Peter felt better that they were out of the snow. 'I wonder how far this goes,' he said and his query was quickly answered. They were soon back in the snow and his headlights were picking up larger and larger snowflakes. Again, the amount of snow on the road surface was getting deeper. Peter commented that the road seemed to be climbing. 'I don't think it's anything too severe. After all, we're still being passed by everyone else.'

They immediately disappeared into another tunnel.

'Many more of these and perhaps we won't have to worry about snow on the road,' he chuckled.

This tunnel was much longer.

'I saw a sign indicating it was about three kilometres long,' said Sue.

They were out in the snow again but in front there were orange flashing lights. 'Looks like Christmas lights ahead.' The other traffic had slowed down.

'Peter, I think we've found snow ploughs again. There's not so much snow on the road here,' said Sue.

She was right. Obviously, snow ploughs were clearing a path ahead.

On they drove and they soon saw a signpost for Bischofshofen.

'That's where that border policeman said he came from,' said Sue.

Their speed had dropped to around 50 km – around 30 mph. The road was still climbing but it wasn't too steep. The mountains, which had obviously been on either side, seemed to move away and in the distance, they could see the twinkling lights of habitation.

'Peter, do you think that could be our village? Looking at the map, it's about right,' said Sue, and just as she said it, they saw the signpost – *Altenmarkt*.

'We've made it, Sue! Can't say I'm not pleased. That snow is really heavy now. We'd better take the next slip road off the motorway and hope the roads in the village are cleared as well as this motorway.'

Peter glanced at the illuminated dials on the dashboard. The temperature was now -7 degrees. They had covered 719 miles from Calais. *Wow! It certainly hadn't seemed that far*, thought Peter.

They approached Altenmarkt over a railway crossing. 'Well, at least we could leave by train if things get really bad,' said Peter, laughing.

As they drove through the main village street, Sue spotted a sign for the tourist office.

'Right, let's head for that. They can give us directions to the hotel,' said Peter.

'What a splendid, ultra-modern building,' commented Sue.

Snow, Snow and More Snow!

'Look at all that lovely carved woodwork. Oh, Peter, let me come in with you. This is really exciting.'

They parked outside the tourist office, went in and the heat immediately hit them. The walls and ceilings were wood, the floors tiled and there were lots of plants.

'*Guten Tag,*' said the lady behind the desk. She was exquisitely dressed in local Austrian costume. '*Bitte, kann ich Ihnen helfen?*'

Peter asked if she spoke English. 'Of course,' she said, offended that anyone could think otherwise.

Peter said they were looking for the hotel Lug Ins Land.

'One moment, please,' said the lady and she disappeared into a back office.

A few minutes later, she returned accompanied by a smartly dressed man.

'Hello,' he said. 'Are you Mr Kingston and partner from England? A journalist I think. We are expecting you. I am the tourist director. My name is Kocher.'

Peter was really impressed. 'Yes, that's right. I'm going to write about British people having their Christmas holidays here and what children think about a white Christmas. This is my partner, Sue. She's going to take pictures for my paper and she's also doing a picture feature for her own magazine in London.'

'How do you do,' said Herr Kocher. 'Now, I shall telephone to your hotel and say you have arrived. It is easy to find and I would like to join you in about one hour for a welcoming drink and to give you some information about our resort. Is that satisfactory?'

Peter and Sue both nodded.

Herr Kocher reached across the counter and produced a map of the village. 'We are here, the hotel Lug Ins Land is here. Just five minutes' drive. But, please, be careful of the roads. This snow is now falling on top of hard, packed snow. Here in Altenmarkt our winters last from the end of November, usually until the early part of April, so there is snow and ice on the small road leading to your hotel. I hope you have chains? If so, may I suggest you fit them to your car as the road to the front door of the Lug Ins Land is up a steep slope and you will certainly need chains to arrive.'

Peter assured him he did.

'Right, then I will see you later. I am sure you are going to enjoy your stay.'

Peter and Sue thanked him. Outside, Sue said. 'What really nice people. We could have been anyone. Fancy the director coming out to greet us. I'm really impressed with Austrian hospitality and we've only just arrived.'

They drove down the village main road. 'Just look at the shops; look at the clothes. Just look at all those lovely white fairy lights in the trees and around the roofs of the buildings. They are twinkling through the falling snow. Oh, Peter, isn't this romantic,' she said, leaning over and clutching his arm.

'Steady on, Sue. At this rate, I'll either be arrested or have a crash. Wait until we get to the hotel then you can give me a big hug.'

It was obvious they were not going to reach the hotel without putting on the chains. They had left the main village street and were certainly on a secondary road.

'That must be the swimming pool. The hotel's only just up here,' said Peter. 'I can use the lights from the swimming pool building to get the chains on.' As he tackled the task, Peter was surprised by just how easy the snow chains were to fit. The man at the company in Whitstable had told him to hold them out in front, stretch them apart and just slot them over the tyre and pull the tension chain. It was really as simple as that.

'Why are you putting them on the front wheels?' asked Sue.

'Because the car is front-wheel drive and chains go on the front driving wheels,' said Peter, as though everyone, including Sue, should know that.

Chains fitted, they set off once again.

'What's that clonking noise?' asked Sue with a worried expression.

'I probably haven't tightened them up enough. Don't worry; I can see to it tomorrow. At least we should now be able to reach the hotel front door, unless you want to carry the luggage from here?'

The travel agent had not been joking when he said it was a steep climb up to the hotel. The snow was thick on the swerving driveway, but Peter's car, helped by the chains, had ample power to make it to the top.

The Lug Ins Land was built in the old Austrian style, substantially of wood and three-floors high. As they got out of the car, the front door opened and a man with a white beard, dressed in traditional lederhosen, strode over.

'Mr Kingston, I think. My name is Heinz Schenk: Heinz to everyone. Welcome to our little hotel. Please leave your luggage and come and have a warm drink. I would like to introduce you to my wife, Anita. I think you are in for a surprise!'

From the front entrance lobby, they climbed the stairs and went through a door, which led into a lounge. In the corner was a huge log fire. They were greeted by a lady, who was obviously Anita, dressed in a wonderful, deep-green, traditional, long-flowing skirt and white embroidered top.

'Hello. You must be Mr Kingston. And this is?'

Peter introduced Sue.

'If you don't mind me saying, you don't sound Austrian,' said Sue.

'Anita is Welsh,' chimed in Heinz with a grin. 'Sit down and have a glass of Glühwein. It's just the drink to warm you up on a cold evening,' he said.

The hot, spiced Glühwein certainly warmed them up as they told Heinz and Anita about their journey.

'You have done well to arrive now. We have a lot of snow coming for the next two days, but that will not stop people skiing,' said Heinz.

Peter told them it was his first visit to Austria. No, he had never been skiing before, although Sue had been once with her school a long time ago. 'We went to a small French village by bus and I didn't enjoy it very much then,' she said.

After a second glass of Glühwein, Anita said she would show

them to their room. Heinz reminded them that the tourist director was coming later. 'I think you have time to wash and change. It's a very busy time at the tourist office, but Herr Kocher is always interested in meeting journalists.'

Their room was on the second floor and from the window they could see the lights of the village. It was en suite with shower and a separate toilet. All the furniture was constructed of heavy wood. 'No shortage of raw materials around here,' commented Peter.

Sue tried the bed. It was springy and covered with a large duvet.

'Come on, Sue. That tourist office director will be here soon and we had better not keep him waiting. You have a quick wash first while I unpack my suitcase.'

Half an hour later, they were back down in the lounge. Some other guests had appeared. They must have been British because Peter could hear them speaking English.

Herr Kocher had ordered a bottle of red wine. 'I drink to your good health and to a pleasant stay here in our region,' he said.

Peter and Sue raised their glasses.

Herr Kocher produced an impressive folder. 'This is our information pack for journalists. You will find the information in English. I have included colour slides, but I know you wish to take your own. Also, you will find a complimentary ski pass for each of you from our lift company.'

Peter thanked him and complimented him on his English.

'I had a good teacher. My wife is from Canada; we met on the world cup circuit,' he said.

Peter and Sue were further impressed. 'You mean you were an international skier?' asked Sue.

Heinz, who had joined them, said. 'Better than that; Edi Kocher is a former Austrian champion. Our village is very proud of its hero.'

Herr Kocher looked suitably embarrassed. 'It was a long time ago; now I work for a living,' he said with a smile.

Heinz said dinner would be ready in ten minutes. Peter looked at his watch; it was already 7.30 p.m. Herr Kocher said Peter should come to the office if he needed anything. 'Perhaps it would be in order for my wife and myself to join the two of you for dinner on Friday. She likes to use her language and speak to British people,' he commented and with that, he said his farewells.

Peter and Sue went into the dining room. Individual lamps illuminated the tables, most of which already had guests seated at them. A few people said, 'Good evening,' others just glanced. Anita showed them to a table at the far end in a small alcove and said, 'Heinz does all the cooking. I have two waitresses who help me with the meals and in the bar. Now what would you like to drink?'

Peter and Sue thought a beer would be appropriate after all that Glühwein and red wine, and went on to order a substantial meal: a thick vegetable soup, followed by goulash and dumplings with plenty of vegetables, and apple strudel with custard for dessert. After they had eaten, Anita said they could either have coffee at the table or in the lounge. They opted for the lounge, in which there were several couples with children and one family who invited Sue and Peter to join them.

Anita came in with the coffee and introduced Hazel and John Young. Everyone shook hands.

'I hear you are a journalist,' said John.

Peter explained the purpose of the visit.

'Are these your children?' he enquired.

Hazel called over Robert, who was nine, and his sister, Rebecca, eleven. They both politely said, 'Hello,' and then went back over to an adjoining table where they were playing snakes and ladders.

'They love skiing,' said Hazel. 'This is our fourth visit here to Altenmarkt. Have you been here before?'

Peter said they hadn't but it had been recommended by a travel agent. 'In fact, I haven't skied before,' he said.

'Shame on you,' said John. 'You will be like the rest of us and get bitten by the bug. Then you won't be able to get enough skiing.'

Peter asked politely where they came from.

'Westerham,' said Hazel. 'It's just off the M25 in Kent. Do you know it?'

'Know it,' said Peter. 'I work on the local paper at Tonbridge, so you could say we're neighbours.'

'What a small world,' commented Hazel. 'You see that family sitting over there with the two little girls. They come from Tunbridge Wells – but remember to mention the "Royal". They like everyone to be reminded of the town's full name,' said John with a laugh and called them over. 'This young chap is a reporter from the paper at Tonbridge. He's here to write about the place,' said John.

The second man introduced himself. 'Philip Browne – with an "e". My wife, Pippa. The girls are Samantha, six, and Sue-Ellen, seven.'

Peter made a mental note. 'Look, I know we've just arrived, but I've got to get an article done and my partner, Sue, is taking pictures. As you come from our area, it would be just perfect to feature you all. That is, if you don't mind?' asked Peter.

Both couples said they wouldn't mind.

Just then, Heinz came in, still wearing his chef's coat. 'I hope the meal was alright. We get really traditional on Christmas Day with turkey and all the trimmings. Otherwise, our guests like traditional Austrian food.'

Peter and Sue said they were easy to please. 'When in Rome and all that,' said Peter.

They then chatted about the UK and why the couples came away at Christmas.

'To be honest, old chap,' said Philip, 'it's a lot cheaper to come here than to spend Christmas at home. Besides, the girls love playing in the snow. Think of all the food you have to buy for the Christmas and New Year period. Then there is entertaining of family and friends, plus gas, electricity, etc. The list is endless. And besides, it is just work, work and more work for the wife.'

John and Hazel agreed. 'We couldn't contemplate spending Christmas at home now. No cooking, no washing up and the children simply love it. They have ski school from ten until midday. Then we meet for a snack lunch and they're out on the slopes from two until half past three. Then we all go for a cup of hot chocolate,' said Hazel.

'We came down overnight Saturday and got here yesterday lunchtime. The kids sleep naturally at night and the roads are so quiet. We got here before it started to snow,' said John.

Philip said they had caught a Friday evening ferry but basically done the same. 'We wanted to see the Christmas market in Munich, so we spent a few hours there on Saturday afternoon before getting here Saturday evening,' said Philip.

Peter listened attentively, but it was gone 9.00 p.m. and he and Sue felt weary. It had been a long day, especially driving in that snow, so they eventually said their goodnights and went to their room.

'What a day. I'm absolutely whacked out,' said Peter, dropping onto the bed. 'Not too tired I hope,' said Sue with that glint in her eye.

What I do for England, thought Peter and after shedding their clothes, they scrambled under the duvet. Bliss!

6

All Work and No Play Makes . . .

Their lovemaking had been passionate but short-lived. Both were too tired for anything else and they had slept like logs. Sue was the first to wake.

'Peter, it's already eight twenty and breakfast is between eight thirty and nine.'

Peter grunted and turned over.

'Oh, Peter, come on! We don't want to be last down to breakfast like newlyweds! People will start talking.'

Peter opened one eye. Sue, as always, looked lovely. Really sexy.

'No, Peter, not now. It's time for breakfast. Wait until tonight. It'll be much more enjoyable,' and with that she was out of bed and into the bathroom.

Peter heard the shower running and after reminding himself he was really here to work, gently eased himself out of bed. He drew back the curtains, saw that it was still snowing and there had been a lot of snow overnight. *Probably more than 12 inches*, thought Peter, looking down at the ground.

Sue came out of the shower with a towel wrapped round her. Peter made a grab for it but missed.

'Peter Kingston. Really, I'm beginning to think you're a sex-starved maniac.'

'Only when it comes to you, Sue darling. I've got a lot of lost ground to make up.'

Sue told him it would certainly not be before breakfast so he disappeared into the shower.

Most people were already down to breakfast and heads turned. Heinz was there and greeted them. 'Good morning. I hope you slept well.'

'Like a log,' said Sue. 'It must be the mountain air.' They made their way over to their usual table and Heinz came across.

'Coffee? Help yourself to the breakfast buffet. You will find cereals, yoghurt, home-cooked meats, local cheeses and homemade jams. There are also hot bread rolls from our local bakery.'

Peter and Sue helped themselves to fresh orange juice and cereal, after which they put some meat and cheese on their plates.

'If it's like this each morning, I'll go home looking like a barrel,' commented Sue.

'Let's not talk about you going home just yet. We've only just arrived. Make hay while the sun shines,' said Peter.

Heinz came back with the coffee. 'It's going to snow for the rest of the day so not much fun taking pictures. Anyway, if it's alright with the two of you, I'll take you to the local slopes this morning so you can get a feel for the place. The main skiing is a short drive up the valley. I suppose you know we have one hundred and fourteen lifts linking four valleys and covering three hundred and twenty kilometres of skiing area.'

Peter assured him he did. 'It's a bit difficult to take it all in yet. But a trip to the village slopes would be great. I need some atmosphere before I can start writing. Sue can get her pictures when the sun comes out. I suppose the *sun will* come out?' he asked.

Heinz said the weather forecast was a little better for tomorrow. 'We have the same trouble here as you do in England. The weather bureau occasionally gets it wrong.' After breakfast, Peter studied the information in his press folder. Certainly, it seemed a huge area for skiing but Peter was really interested in what there was for the children. As he browsed, John and Hazel came into the lounge with Robert and Rebecca. They were all done up in colourful ski clothing. Mum and Dad were in matching anoraks and trousers, the children were both in one-piece ski suits with matching pom pom hats.

'My, you all look very smart,' remarked Sue. 'Where are you off to for your skiing? I'd like to get some pictures later.'

John said that, as it was snowing, they would go to the local slopes.

'It's called HoBi for short. They have a very good ski school for the children there and very gentle slopes for beginners. It's only about five minutes in the car from here and Heinz will show you where to find us,' said Hazel.

That suited Peter and Sue very nicely. Shame it was still snowing. Some blue sky and sunshine would enhance the colours of the ski clothing.

A little later, after they had put on their snow boots and anoraks, Heinz reappeared to take them out. 'I will show you some of the local places so you can get a feel for the atmosphere and size of the area. Even though it's Christmas and one of our busiest times, you will not notice the people because they have so much room and so many lifts to use,' he told them.

First of all they went to HoBi. Lots of children were milling about.

'Ski school starts at ten a.m. The ski school director usually likes classes of no more than eight children. It is more manageable for the instructor,' said Heinz.

Sue asked about the type of instructor.

'Many of the instructors come from this region. They must all be exceptionally good skiers and hold a full Austrian ski teachers' certificate. For the children, the instructors can be both male and female, but we find the young ladies are very good for the children,' said Heinz. He told them it was necessary for all instructors to speak several languages. 'Of course, English is usually the second language because it is a language widely used.'

Next, they drove further up the valley to a place called Zauchensee. Heinz explained it was the main ski station.

'We have gondolas and chairlifts setting off in different directions and we can transport many thousands of skiers every hour. You can begin here and ski the four valleys. You must be a good skier and it takes the whole day, but many of our guests do it.'

'What is that large expanse of white?' asked Sue, pointing.

Heinz explained it was a large frozen lake. 'It is full of trout because Zauchensee is a summer resort as well. People come for walking holidays, as well as fishing. It is lovely also in summer,' said Heinz, beaming.

Peter was making copious notes.

Heinz then showed them two separate ski schools for children. One embraced a Walt Disney cartoon set: an Indian wigwam and a large wheel with a pole. 'You see,' said Heinz, 'when children have to learn to stand on their skis, they hold onto that pole and the wheel goes round. The children simply slide and they soon learn to balance.'

Sue asked about the Walt Disney characters.

'It is important for children to enjoy their skiing from the beginning. Some do not like at first to leave mums and dads. But the instructors are trained to quickly make the children feel at home. They can all relate to Mickey Mouse and the other characters. After forty-five minutes, skiing stops, they go into that hut, which is heated, and have a warm drink, usually hot chocolate, and they sit and listen to a story. It is important the children do not get too tired, or cold,' said Heinz.

Sue and Peter were most impressed.

'I must get some pictures,' said Sue.

'Okay. But the weather will get better after tomorrow,' said Heinz.

Undaunted, Sue got out of the car.

While she was taking pictures, Peter heard that Heinz was a member of the mountain rescue team. 'Safety is paramount in the mountains. The slopes must be in good condition and when we have heavy falls of snow as we do now, then we must ensure there are no avalanches.'

Peter was amazed to see tracked vehicles going up an incline, which looked at least a one in three slope.

'Those are the piste machines. They usually work at night but when it is snowing they work all day as well, just smoothing and compressing down the snow so that the slopes are in a good condition for the skiers,' said Heinz.

Sue got back in the car. 'That made some good pictures, Peter. Even without the sun, the colours of the children's ski clothing really looked good. They all seem to be enjoying themselves.'

They set off back down the valley and Peter asked if they could stop at HoBi and find the other English families. When they arrived, the three of them got out and they soon spotted John and Hazel with their children. Pippa also came over with Sue-Ellen and Samantha.

Heinz asked Peter and Sue if they would like a hot chocolate. 'Even out here on the slopes you can get a warm drink,' he told them and disappeared in the direction of a small wooden chalet.

Philip Browne then appeared. 'Well, what do you think of it so far?' he asked.

'Absolutely great,' said Peter and Sue, more or less in unison.

'I can see why you come here,' said Sue. She took some general pictures and then asked if she could have a family photo. 'This will be for Peter's article. I have more time to get pictures for my magazine feature,' she said.

Heinz called them over. 'Three hot chocolates!'

Peter asked where Heinz had learned to speak such good English. 'It's a long story, but in Wales.'

'In Wales!' exclaimed Peter. 'What were you doing in Wales?'

Heinz said that was part of the long story, but it was where he had met his wife, Anita.

'She has been here for over thirty-five years and is very much Austrian now. But she keeps her roots in Wales and we do get a lot of visitors from there both summer and winter,' he said.

'Well I never,' said Sue. 'What a lovely story.'

After they had finished their hot chocolate, Heinz asked if they wanted to stay or go back to the hotel with him. 'You can walk from here in about fifteen minutes to the Lug Ins Land. But as it is still snowing and is quite cold, you may wish to come back now,' he said.

Peter wanted to start on his feature. After all, he would have to send it back by Friday and he needed to do some more research, so he agreed to return with Heinz. During the short drive back, via the village, Heinz showed them places where they could get a midday snack. 'You will find a bowl of soup with a thick slice of our locally made bread is more than sufficient at lunchtime,' he told them.

Back in their hotel room, Peter switched on his laptop and started the outline of his very first travel feature. He had so much material to include in his first article, including kids in the snow with real Christmas trees and horse-drawn sleighs with bells jingling from the horse's necks. *What a lovely angle*, thought Peter.

Later, they took the advice of Heinz and made their way to the village centre where they sat at a window seat in a small café in the village centre. There was a charming church with a very tall, steep spire to one side, an impressive ice-carving on another corner and a row of three horse-drawn sleighs outside.

'Oh, Peter, let's hire one of those while we're here. How romantic. I'm going to get some pictures as soon as I see anyone getting in one of those.'

Peter thought it better to wait until it stopped snowing. 'I'm sure it must be more pleasant when the sun is shining!'

Sue decided Peter was right and would wait until the morning.

'Do you realise it's Christmas Day tomorrow? What have you got for me, Peter?'

Peter told her she had better wait until the morning. 'I'm not sure I told Father Christmas where you were this year,' he said, pulling her leg, and Sue pretended to be really hurt.

'Short rations for you tonight, Peter Kingston.'

Peter decided to ignore the remark. After all, he knew she didn't really mean it – or did she?

That evening, after dinner, they sat in the lounge chatting to the other English families and watching the CNN worldwide news. Suddenly, there was a news flash and the presenter said that CNN were immediately going over to their London desk. Peter and the others stopped talking and watched, Peter's mouth opening wider and wider as the news presenter told them a notorious, international drugs smuggler had escaped while being moved from a London courthouse to a high security prison on the Isle of Wight. The television showed a picture of Nigel Ewell.

'I don't believe it!' said Peter, turning to Sue. 'I was at his first court case just a few weeks ago. It seemed he had run down a crime reporter colleague of mine from the same newspaper group and after a car chase, the police had captured him in a cul de sac in the centre of Tonbridge. His case was then moved to London because he was wanted by customs on the serious drug-smuggling charges. There were some ugly-looking, quite unfriendly characters in the court room staring at journalists, including me. It was intimidating in a strange way,' Peter told the other guests.

Everyone was now glued to the television. The CNN reporter was speaking live from a road in Hampshire, explaining that the prison van had been hijacked, later found abandoned with the three security officers badly beaten and now in hospital, but there was no sign of Nigel Ewell.

It was believed a helicopter had been used, but radar had lost it over the Channel. Interpol had been contacted and a search was now on in Northern France for the escaped prisoner and any signs of the helicopter.

They all looked at each other as the remainder of the CNN news continued.

Peter said to the gathering, 'I may not be a crime reporter, but if I know this villain, Ewell, this has been planned at the highest level and there will be no chance of the police catching him. My bet is he will be spirited away to South America where his drugs empire is probably run from. I'm glad I'm out here and off the case. I bet there are some red faces amongst the police and the security firm. So much for privatisation. It was much better, and safer, when the police themselves transferred high-risk prisoners like Ewell. This is not the first time this particular private security firm has lost a prisoner. There have also been escapes from privately run prisons. What a mess.'

Sue asked him if he now felt better getting that off his chest. Everyone else laughed and Pippa Browne said, 'Forget it. You're here to enjoy yourself. I thought you were writing a travel feature not turning into an investigative crime reporter.'

Peter agreed, Heinz passed round a bottle of red wine and the two mums said they would check on the children upstairs.

'They are so excited it's Christmas. They keep asking if Santa Claus remembers they are here in Austria,' said Pippa. 'I keep trying to reassure them but you know what kids are like.'

Peter said he thought it was not only kids who wanted to know if Father Christmas had remembered. Sue gave him a gentle kick under the table and Peter laughed. 'Wait and see,' he commented without looking directly at Sue, but winking to the others.

Heinz asked if anyone was interested in attending the midnight mass. They all thought it better to have an early night.

After going to their room, they talked for a while, mainly about Peter's feature, and he reminded her that she was preparing a picture feature as well. But, Sue said, hers could wait until she got back after New Year. And then all thoughts of work fell away and they were passionate in their lovemaking. Everything just seemed so perfect. It had been a long time since Peter had felt so happy. He and Sue just seemed to be right for each other.

Peter and Sue woke to the sound of church bells summoning villagers, and perhaps a few holidaymakers, to the 8.00 a.m. service.

'It's stopped snowing,' said Sue, gently pulling back the curtains. 'Peter, look at that wonderful sky; it's going to be such a lovely day.'

Peter had carefully put Sue's Christmas card and present under the bed on his side. She came and sat on the bed next to him.

'Well, has Father Christmas been or must I go and find myself a more reliable man?' she asked.

Peter looked at her. What wonderful eyes she had, tinged with a slight green. They seemed to sparkle like emeralds. Her body was just perfect and wonderfully outlined through her transparent nightie.

'Peter!' She brought him back to reality. 'Are you concentrating?'

Oh yes, thought Peter. *I'm concentrating. Breakfast isn't until nine o'clock. Might as well enjoy some more of this lovely lady.*

He pulled her gently over onto the bed and gave her a long, lingering kiss, his hand moving slowly and gently over her small, firm, rounded breasts.

'Father Christmas says you have to earn your present,' he said, laughing. And with that, he pulled the duvet over them and they became entwined in bliss once more.

Half an hour must have passed before they came up for air.

'Peter, I'm so happy. Two weeks ago none of this seemed remotely possible. It's as good as being on honeymoon.'

Honeymoon! Peter bounced back to reality. Was this the way Sue's mind was working? Was everything going too fast? He decided to ignore the remark for the moment and reached down to retrieve the present and card from the floor. Handing it to her, he said. 'This is for the most wonderful lady in my life. Happy Christmas, Sue.'

She pulled excitedly at the wrapping paper to reveal a long, black box. Opening it, she saw the most perfect two-strand necklace.

'I hope you like it,' said Peter.

'Like it. Peter, darling, it's lovely. It's something I've always wanted. You're a clever man to know the way to a girl's heart!'

Sue opened the card. It was romantic in its simplicity. *To the only girl in my heart*, it read.

Without saying anything, she put her arms around his neck and gave him a kiss.

Slowly pulling himself away, Peter enquired, 'Is it too much to expect Father Christmas might have visited me also?'

Sue got out of bed, went to the wardrobe and opened her suitcase. She came back carrying a fairly large parcel with a card fixed to the outside.

Peter opened the card. *To the one I love.* The message was enough.

He opened the parcel. It was certainly an item of clothing as it was soft and floppy: a blue pullover with a rounded neck, perfect for outdoor life in the mountains.

'Thank you, Sue. That's a really sensible present. And the size is right as well.'

Sue told him she had asked his mother, just to make certain.

They showered and went down to breakfast and were pleased to see they were not the last.

Heinz wished everyone a Happy Christmas and said horse-drawn sleigh rides were available that morning. He told them that, based on four sharing, it worked out at around £5.00 per person. Peter and Sue thought they could afford £20.00 to have one to themselves. Heinz said he would book it for 11.00 a.m. and told Sue she should take her camera as the ride would be through the forest and out across the fields towards the next village of Radstadt.

Before setting off, Peter phoned home to wish his parents a Happy Christmas. His mother was overjoyed at hearing from him and wanted to ask so many questions. Peter told her firmly that he had to keep the call short, but he was fine, having an interesting time and would send a card. His father said Christmas would never be the same again but looked forward to seeing his son's first travel article in print.

They had a perfect morning, with Sue taking pictures of everything, from Peter standing by the horses with the driver, to people on cross country skis and children pulling sledges. Peter was amazed by the wide range of colours out on the slopes: the reds, blues, greens and yellows of the anoraks, various colours of pom pom hats and even ski trousers came in different colours. Peter thought it might have been safety: a skier in a brightly coloured outfit would be easier to spot against the white snow. Sue thought it was probably something to do with changing fashions.

After a snack lunch back in the village, they returned to their room so that Peter could finish his feature. He wanted to be able to send it first thing Friday morning. He read it through and was pleased with the result. Sue then read it and said the editor should be equally pleased.

'Considering it's your first travel piece, I think it's really good. It certainly brings home the message that mums and dads should consider taking their kids away at Christmas to a snow-covered country like Austria,' she said.

Downstairs in the lounge, there was the usual log fire burning and Anita had prepared homemade cake and Austrian chocolate biscuits with a slight taste of ginger, to be enjoyed with a choice of tea or coffee. The other guests came in and everyone remarked on how wonderful it had been to see the sunshine.

Heinz came over and said to Sue, 'I saw our local photographer at lunchtime. He says the newspaper office at Bischofshofen has a facility to send pictures to anywhere in Europe by downloading your pictures from the digital photo card. I can give you and Peter directions and you can drive over there tomorrow.'

They thanked Heinz. He was really turning out to be a gem. Everyone in this picturesque village seemed so friendly.

The next day, they made their way over to Bischofshofen. The roads were beautifully clear of snow and Peter had taken the chains off before they set out. Heinz had telephoned ahead and they were greeted at the newspaper office by Fritz Gueller, the deputy editor. He invited them for a tour of the building.

'We are preparing tomorrow's edition. Our newspaper covers the whole region and is published daily,' he said. Editions comprised national and international news, but as much local news as possible, he told them.

Peter was impressed and said his group had a daily, several weeklies and a monthly colour magazine. Things happened slightly differently in England, although their daily also carried regional as well as national news.

They drank coffee in an upstairs room and Peter was interested to hear that the escape of Nigel Ewell was even considered a story worth using.

'We are a little surprised your authorities in England can have such lax security that a notorious criminal can escape while being taken to prison,' said Fritz Gueller. Then, changing the subject, he asked if they had ever seen ski jumping.

Peter and Sue said that, apart from on television, they had not.

'Well, you must come as this newspaper's guests at New Year. Bischofshofen is famous for its ski jump. We are part of what is called the Four Hills Championships. This year should be excellent because we have such good snow conditions. The weather will stay cold but dry with sunshine. There will be some long jumps this year,' he said.

Peter and Sue thanked Herr Gueller for his hospitality and said they would be there early on New Year's Day.

He told them jumping started at 9.30 a.m. and they remembered it was a thirty-minute drive.

'An early start. Not too much merrymaking New Year's Eve,' remarked Sue.

Both knew that Sue was scheduled to fly from Salzburg to Gatwick the day after New Year's and neither wanted to remind themselves. They still had several days to enjoy each other before it was time to part.

7

Time to Move on

The ski jumping at Bischofshofen had been spectacular, with men flying through the air like birds. There had been one or two fallers, but nobody had been seriously hurt. Much to the delight of the huge crowd, estimated at over 10,000, an Austrian had won. He had been second a few days before at Garmisch-Partenkirchen and now led the Four Hills Championship.

For Sue and Peter, it was a remarkable day. Sue's pictures had been downloaded by computer and sent back by satellite to the UK. Some would accompany Peter's first travel article. Back in Altenmarkt, they had taken a horse-drawn sleigh ride to the neighbouring town of Radstadt, across snow-covered fields and through a pine forest, silent but for the sound of the horses and the sleigh sliding effortlessly over the deep snow.

That evening in the hotel, Heinz had prepared a special meal with a bottle of an excellent Austrian red wine with his compliments for the couple. Although Peter still had a few more days in Altenmarkt, it was not going to be the same without Sue and he would have to immerse himself heavily in work.

They spent an hour chatting in the lounge to the other guests, who wished Sue a safe journey back to the UK. Heinz had agreed to take her to Salzburg Airport but it was to be an early start. The flight was at 8.50 a.m., so they would be leaving the hotel at 7.00 a.m. Heinz had said they should allow forty minutes for the journey.

That night, Peter and Sue made love twice. Little was said. Actions spoke louder than words. But the next morning, during the journey with Heinz, Peter promised to keep in touch with Sue at least twice a week. He reminded her that he was in Kitzbühel next and would ring her as soon as he arrived in his hotel.

At the airport, neither wanted a tearful goodbye. Heinz had stayed with the car and as waiting was limited to thirty minutes, Peter promised not to be long. At the departure gate he gave Sue a long, warm embrace and she promised not to cry.

'Peter, I've had such a wonderful and unforgettable time. Take care of yourself and I envy you the coming weeks, moving to all the wonderful ski resorts. But don't go looking for any glamorous new photographers to take my place.'

Peter told her not to be so silly. 'I'm sure the tourist offices will find someone to provide me with pictures.'

It was time to go. The flight was called. Peter and Sue pulled apart. She only glanced back once and was gone. Peter walked slowly back to the waiting car and climbed in. Heinz knew better than to say anything at first. They were well on their way back from Salzburg towards Altenmarkt before Heinz said, 'I have arranged something special for later today. I am going to show you how our mountain rescue unit works and how we control the risk of avalanches.'

Anything to take his mind off Sue! For the first time, his life really seemed empty.

The next few days passed quickly and Peter allowed himself to become immersed in his writing. He had a long meeting with Edi Kocher, who rang to the tourist director in Kitzbühel. After a short time, Herr Kocher put down the phone and told Peter all was arranged. He would be met at the tourist office and shown to his hotel.

'It is quite different from Altenmarkt,' said Edi Kocher. 'Kitzbühel is a famous old, walled town and even more famous for its Hahnenkamm downhill race.'

Peter assured Herr Kocher that any place would have to go a long way to beat Altenmarkt and the surrounding mountains. 'I have been so impressed, not only with the warmth of my welcome, but with my introduction into winter sports. I am sure Sue and myself will be back privately for a skiing holiday next winter,' he said.

Back at the Lug Ins Land, Heinz had a surprise for him.

'I have just received this by fax from England. I think you will be pleased.'

Peter took the several sheets of paper. It was his travel article. Wow! His name in lights! The office had reduced it down and it still covered three sheets. Although the photos were a little black, Sue had obviously also been rewarded for her hard work. There was a short, *Well done, keep them coming* message from the editor. Peter decided he would look at his article online later when he was back on his computer.

'I took the liberty of reading what you had written,' said Heinz to Peter. 'You have put Altenmarkt well and truly on the map and I like the sounds of your writing. I am sure Edi Kocher will be also pleased.'

Heinz agreed to make a photocopy and deliver it to the tourist office. 'I have just said my goodbyes, so I think it would be better if you gave him the copy,' said Peter.

Heinz and Anita helped Peter with his luggage. He had already said goodbye to the other guests, who were also departing the following day. A second photocopy had been made to show to the other families, especially as all were featured both in pictures and words.

Heinz told Peter the journey to Kitzbühel would not take longer than two hours. 'The roads are clear and it is a pleasant car ride without any steep hills or mountain passes to negotiate,' said Heinz.

Then it was time to leave with a promise from Peter that he would be back. Heinz and Anita smiled. They knew Peter meant it.

8

Caught in the Spider's Web

Peter's drive to Kitzbühel had been uneventful. His greeting at the tourist office, right in the heart of the old, walled town had been equally as warm as in Altenmarkt. He had experienced a slight brush with the local police when he tried to park in the wrong place. But the polite policeman had redirected him to a car park not too far away, reminding him guests were always welcome in Kitzbühel, providing they observed the law. Only taxis and horse-drawn sleighs were allowed to park within the walled town.

Peter's hotel was different again from the Lug Ins Land. It was modern but still retained some Austrian charm. It had been constructed six years before, according to the tourist director, Herr Schaffer, to meet the growing demand from tourists. The Hotel Buchlhof was on the outskirts of the town and had been constructed alongside a much older building, which had obviously been the original guesthouse but was now an annex to the new hotel.

Peter booked in and was shown to his room. A porter had helped him with his luggage from the car and details in four European languages in the bedroom informed him that dinner was at 7.00 p.m.

Having unpacked and changed into his warm outdoor clothes and snow boots, Peter made his way down to reception. There, a small group of men were also booking in. One in the centre with a beard looked vaguely familiar, reminding Peter of someone back home, although he couldn't place exactly who.

The sun was slowly sinking behind the tops of the mountains as Peter walked through the deep, crisp snow, looking at his local map, trying to identify which one was the famous Hahnenkamm. Two horse-drawn sleighs filled with happy, laughing holidaymakers passed him as he made his way back towards the walled town.

Peter was amazed by the selection of shops. They ranged from the traditional souvenir shops to those selling locally cured meats. Clothing shops were numerous and many displayed elegant outfits for ladies, including fur coats and fur hats. However, Peter thought it unlikely that such displays of fur would be welcomed back in the UK.

Back at the hotel, Peter put the finishing touches to his second article, which included the ski jumping at Bischofshofen, then soaked in a nice warm bath and dressed for dinner. This hotel was slightly more formal than he had been used to in Altenmarkt, so as a new arrival he thought he had better try and make a good impression.

Dinner was good: a thick pea soup followed by slices of toast with fish and a main meal of meat and three veg. Dessert was peaches or, as an option, some local cheese, which Peter decided would be a better choice.

As he sat in the lounge close to a blazing log fire, he again spotted the men he had first seen in reception. Certainly the one with the beard did look familiar, but from where? It had to be too much of a coincidence that they also came from England. They weren't looking in his direction, so he decided to put himself out of his misery. He strolled out to reception and asked the young Austrian girl if she had some information on local places of interest. She produced two leaflets: one on a water sports centre, which she said was extremely popular with guests as it had a swimming pool, sauna and whirlpool and steam room; the other leaflet gave details of a museum and places where you could watch local products being made. There was woodcarving, cheese-making and jewellery from a local mine. Yes, she assured him, mining was still carried out around Kitzbühel. Finally, Peter decided to ask about the other guests.

'Do you have any other guests from Britain staying in the hotel?' he asked.

The girl replied that they did not. 'Most of our guests are from Germany, Switzerland and Holland. There are two hotels in Kitzbühel, which cater extensively for English guests and work with English tour operators. My sister works at one. I will give you the name and perhaps you can visit there tomorrow,' she said.

After enjoying a beer at the bar, Peter made his way to his room, putting out of his mind any more thoughts that he might have known the men in the lounge. He got out his laptop and decided to write a short piece on the history of Kitzbühel as background to his next article, which would be about families who were not reliant on school holiday time for when they could travel abroad.

The next morning, as he sat enjoying a very good breakfast buffet, the tourist director arrived.

'Good morning, Mr Kingston. I have arranged this morning for us to travel to the top of the Hahnenkamm Mountain to meet the director of our lift company and also to meet one of our local race officials. We will have lunch on the mountain and as the weather is very good, you can enjoy excellent views of our town and surrounding valleys. If you like, we can ski down afterwards.'

Peter quickly explained that would not be such a good idea. 'You see, I'm really a novice. This is the first time I have been skiing and at Altenmarkt I barely negotiated a gentle incline. So I don't think coming down a mountain when I can hardly stop on the flat is very sensible.'

Herr Schaffer laughed. 'I agree. So we can have an even better lunch with some more local wine and rely on the cable car to bring us safely down,' he said. 'But I will arrange for you to have some skiing lessons. It is a quiet time now that our New Year and Christmas guests have gone so there is plenty of room at the ski school. You can have one-to-one lessons so you will quickly proceed to become an expert.'

Peter did not really see it like that, but decided not to make any comment.

Lunch was good, very good, and a glass of schnapps before, two glasses of wine with the meal and a tea with rum afterwards gave Peter a glowing feeling. The cable car ride had been spectacular. It had been his first experience in such a huge lift. No fewer than 150 people could be transported in just five minutes from the bottom to the top of the Hahnenkamm Mountain. It was a strange and slightly unnerving feeling when the cable car swung as it passed over the midway pylon. Peter was intrigued as it had slowly and snugly come to rest at the top station. The views had been breath-taking, with clear blue sky and wintry sunshine sparkling off the tops of the mountains.

The tourist director had told Peter that skiing had begun at Kitzbühel in 1892 and the town was steeped in 700 years of history, although traces of its history dated back to the Bronze Age and there had been extensive copper mining in the area. It was just as well Peter had made copious notes before and during lunch. He would never have remembered everything now that he was on his way down in the impressive cable car.

It was agreed that Peter would have a skiing lesson the following morning at 10.00 a.m. and in the afternoon, he would be taken to one of the copper mines in Jochberg, a nearby village. Before that, Peter would take a catnap, followed by a swim at Aquarena and a massage, which would cost about £7.50.

On his way from the cable car station back to the hotel, Peter again saw the men who were staying at his hotel. They did not appear dressed for skiing but showed a slight interest as he passed by on the opposite side of the street, where snow was piled up at least a metre high. Back in his room, Peter was even too tired to get out his laptop. It could wait until later when he had enjoyed a swim and massage and was feeling refreshed before dinner.

He had slept well for an hour, taken a taxi to Aquarena and swum for about thirty minutes while waiting for the clock to show it was time for his massage, which had been booked from his hotel reception. Now back in the hotel and with a beer in front of him, Peter set to work with the laptop. Background research was important to any story, even a travel piece, and this was all about the quietness of a resort with few children around. No wonder so many skiers decided to come when the slopes were less crowded and the kids had all returned to school.

Glancing out of his hotel window, Peter spotted a large, black limousine coming up the hotel driveway: not a taxi and obviously containing someone of importance, but why not stay in one of the resort's famous five-star hotels? Peter craned his neck forward to get a better look. He recognised two of the men already staying at the hotel; the third was a stranger and they quickly went inside. Peter's inquisitive, journalistic mind went into overdrive. The more he thought about it, the more the man with the beard played on his mind. And who was this new guest – or was he a guest? – just arriving. Peter signed off from his laptop and went downstairs. Time for a refill at the bar.

The lounge was relatively quiet. There were just a few guests sitting around. In the far corner were four men, including the one with the beard and the new arrival. They glanced up as Peter entered, but quickly turned away and lowered their voices. Peter asked for the beer to be put on his room bill and sat near the log fire, pretending to read a magazine, which was all in German and which he stood no chance of understanding, apart from the pictures. His journalistic instinct told him there was a story in the making but he had to remind himself that he was in a foreign country and commissioned to write travel features, not to go probing into things he neither understood nor indeed should try and get to the bottom of. So he switched off, flipped a few more pages and, picking up his beer, returned to his room to get ready for dinner.

The rest of the evening was uneventful. There was no sign of the four men, but there was a good film on television and he remembered he had promised to telephone Sue. It was 9.00 p.m., which meant 8.00 p.m. back in London and Sue should be home from work. He dialled from his room and after four rings, the telephone was answered.

'Hello!' Sue's voice sounded so close and Peter had that strange yearning feeling sweep through his body.

'Sue. Hi, it's Peter. How are you?'

'Oh, Peter. How wonderful to hear from you, darling. Are you missing me? I'm missing you. How's Kitzbühel? How's the weather?' The questions came thick and fast.

'Sue, slow down. One thing at a time. I'm fine, the weather's really lovely with clear blue sky and the hotel is very nice.' Peter told her about his ride up in the cable car, about lunch and everything he could remember, but not about the four strange hotel guests. He knew she would tell him it was none of his business and not to get involved in anything.

'Sue, I'm missing you so much. The days are a bit long by myself and although I'm trying to keep myself occupied, the room's a bit lonely with nobody to talk to.'

She told him not to go looking for a shoulder to cry on. 'Just concentrate on work. I saw a copy of your first article. It was really very good and I was quite pleased with my pictures. My magazine's running a picture feature about children's winter clothes and the editor is pleased that I went out to Austria with you.'

They chatted about a few other things but no more about romance, other than Sue hinting that she would try and get a few days leave and fly out to Switzerland where Peter was due to head after a two-day visit to the world famous Austrian Arlberg resort of Lech – famous for royalty and the rich, or so Peter had been warned. But back to the immediate: 'If you're going to Wengen, I looked it up on the map and I could get a flight from Gatwick to Bern. It's a short train ride to Interlaken. We could meet there,' she told him.

Peter promised they could finalise details within the next couple of days and promised to ring her to confirm arrangements. He then gave her his hotel name and telephone number in Lech, just in case.

When Peter came down to breakfast the next morning, there was an overnight fax from his office and a request to ring Bert Maynard. As EU time was an hour ahead of time back in the UK, Peter decided he had time for breakfast first. There was no sign of the four men at breakfast.

Back in his room, Peter's call to his office went through so quickly, it was like telephoning a local shop, and he got through to Bert immediately.

'Hello, Peter. Good to hear from you. Your first article was good stuff and I'm hoping you can send the second one through today. Is it still concentrating on those fortunate adults who can go on holiday more or less when they want to?'

Peter assured him it was. He told Bert the local tourist director had agreed to make some winter pictures available from their website, which could be pulled down at the UK end. Peter gave Bert the web address.

'Peter, you remember that drug smuggler who escaped custody?' It was a statement more than a question because Bert Maynard expected all of his reporters to be up to speed on the news. Peter said he had seen the story on CNN. 'Well, we have had reports that Interpol believe he is somewhere in Europe, so if you get a sniff on anything from any journalists you meet during your travels around Austria or Switzerland in the next few days, let us know. It's still a local story for us.'

Peter said, 'Once a journalist, always a journalist, and while I'm concentrating on tourist articles, if I hear of anything from this end, I will certainly let you know; although I can't imagine the Powder Man or his cronies wanting to be holed up in any of these snow-covered mountain villages,' he said, and went on to tell Bert he was moving on to Lech in the Arlberg region of Austria and after that he would be in Wengen near Interlaken in Switzerland. He would fax the hotel details as soon as he had them and promised Bert the article would be on his desk by the end of the afternoon.

'I have arranged to visit the local newspaper office and they will be sending it through to you,' said Peter. 'Sometimes internet reception in these mountain villages can be a bit hit-and-miss but once I get to Lech-am-Arlberg it should not be such a problem because of the altitude.'

After they had said their goodbyes, Peter put on his skiing clothes and as he arrived at the front door of the hotel, the ski school director arrived to take him for his private lesson.

'Good morning, Mr Kingston. It is a good morning for learning to ski. The snow is firm but not too icy. We will try some gentle slopes near the village so as not to waste time.'

As they drove towards the ski school area, the director informed Peter that he would join him and the Herr Schaffer for lunch. 'I understand you are looking at our copper mine this afternoon. Do you have such mines in England?'

Peter said they had tin mines in Cornwall, which was in the far west of England, and a small gold mine in Wales. 'We did have lots of coal mines but most of these have been closed with the loss of many thousands of jobs.'

The director said it was an unfortunate price for progress and awareness for environmental considerations. 'Natural energy is much better,' he said.

They arrived and Peter got out. There were quite a few people on the slopes and Peter noticed most of them were middle-aged.

'Ah, I see you have noticed our pupils are not children,' smiled the director. 'Most of the people this morning are a little older than you, Mr Kingston. You see, it is never too late to learn to ski. It is a wonderful sport and good exercise for the body. You can enjoy learning to ski without having to go to the top of a mountain. You will see.'

Peter was fitted out with skis and told to walk a few steps. He immediately fell over.

'The first rule of learning to move on skis is to slide the legs. Do not try and walk in the conventional manner by raising one foot after another. Now try again and use the poles to balance yourself . . . Yes, that is better. You see your first successful movement on skis.'

As the morning went on, Peter progressed from moving on level ground to sliding forward on a gentle gradient. He was then shown how to snow plough, a form of controlled forward movement or stopping. Next, he was introduced to a nursery slope lift, which was a continually moving wire with plastic handles.

'Just hold one and allow yourself to be pulled forward,' said the director.

Easier said than done. Peter went over again, but he was encouraged to try again and this time he found himself being gently pulled up the slope. He had been told to let go of the handle at the top. Over he went and managed to quickly move out of the way of the next skier coming up.

The ski school director was alongside him. 'Now we will ski back to the bottom,' he said. 'Remember: push on the knees so your skis are together at the front and apart at the back to form the snowplough position.'

They set off.

'Excellent! Now hold that position. You are doing very well, Mr Kingston.'

They repeated this several times: up to the top and ski back down to the bottom; Peter was whacked!

'I think we should stop and have a coffee,' said the director and Peter readily agreed.

By lunchtime, Peter felt really pleased with himself and was even more pleased when the tourist office director was informed of how quickly he had progressed.

'I think he is – how do you say? – a natural.'

Peter then explained that he had to send his article by the end of the afternoon and asked a few questions about first-time adult skiers. He was told it was not unusual for grandparents to try skiing for the first time. Age is no barrier, just a willingness to learn and to ski within your own capability, he was told. Herr Schaffer told him that many adults in their late twenties and thirties could ski quite well. They preferred coming on holiday in January when there were few children around. 'The slopes are quieter and it is simply a question of preference. Of course, you need to be able to get away so some have not yet started a family; other adults in their early forties have teenage children who can be left at home with grandparents.'

After lunch, it was time for the trip to the mine. Peter thanked the ski school director for the excellent tuition and then set off for the copper mine. It was more of a museum now, but Peter was told that copper had been mined for many centuries. Even in the ninth century BC, records showed that copper was mined and traded over the Alps with Italy.

As the day wore on, they had to get back, but not before Peter had been treated to hot chocolate and some delicious walnut coffee cake – his favourite – by the tourist director.

'Can we meet for dinner this evening? Your hotel, say, seven thirty?' asked Herr Schaffer.

Peter agreed. It would give him enough time to write his article and have a rest and a shower. He certainly needed the rest; he felt really tired after all that skiing. He spent half an hour writing his article and then, having sent it off from the hotel reception, which had better internet reception than his bedroom, he went over to the bed and was quickly asleep. The alarm clock went off at 7.00 p.m., giving Peter half an hour to shower, dress and get in a beer before Herr Schaffer's arrival.

Down in the bar, Peter was one of the first, so he helped himself to a handful of peanuts while his beer was poured. Peter walked over to the log fire from where he could keep an eye on reception for the arrival of Herr Schaffer. He was halfway through his beer when the tourist director arrived.

'What would you like to drink, Herr Schaffer?' asked Peter.

'The same as you, Peter. I can catch up and then we will enjoy a bottle of wine with the meal.'

Over dinner, Peter and the tourist director exchanged pleasantries as well as ideas on what could be of interest in his next article on winter sports and resorts such as Kitzbühel. Herr Schaffer also gave Peter an interesting insight into Kitzbühel's long history, how it became a walled town and how the economy had changed from mining and small industries into the fascinating world of tourism, which now provided this lovely old Austrian town with so much wealth.

'I understand you are moving on to Lech on the Arlberg tomorrow, Peter, and then to Switzerland, so does that mean you have had enough of Austria?' asked Herr Schaffer with a wry smile.

'Not at all,' said Peter and explained that what little he had seen of the country and the people he had met only made him yearn for more. 'I would love to stay longer but during my few months touring around I must see quite a lot of the European Alps, the different countries and how people vary. My articles have to have a different twist each time and maybe even move away from winter sports,' he said, hoping the explanation would be enough.

Herr Schaffer said Peter's short visit to Lech would be fascinating, with fur coats and royalty in abundance. 'But if any European royalty are in Lech, you are unlikely to see much of them as they are closely guarded and slopes are reserved to keep "ordinary guests" well away,' said Herr Schaffer, smiling.

Peter thanked his host for the additional information and with that they retired to the bar for schnapps. Herr Schaffer suggested they enjoy it by the log fire and perhaps extend their conversation on British holiday habits and why so many Brits now wanted to try skiing in the winter. Peter explained that his knowledge on winter sports was still limited, but he was becoming increasingly fascinated the more he saw and the more British people he came into contact with as he toured around.

'I am keen to find out why some Brits prefer one alpine country to another and what the attraction of Switzerland is over Austria,' said Peter, hoping not to offend the tourist director.

'Yes, I do understand, Peter, and perhaps it will be good for me to read your next few articles to see what you have discovered. After all, Austria must not stand still and always expect our guests to come back year after year. Perhaps some, like you, will want to discover if other countries are better, or worse, than we are!'

Soon it was time for the tourist director to bid Peter farewell, but not before Peter promised to arrange for the office to send future copies of his articles. In turn, Herr Schaffer promised Peter any future help he might require. After a firm but polite handshake, it was over and it was 11.15 p.m. already. Peter had an early start so it was time for bed.

As he walked through the hotel lobby, he glanced through the impressive front doors and there again was the black limousine with two men sitting inside, but looking in his direction. *Strange*, thought Peter to himself; his uncanny journalistic sixth sense was beginning to get the better of him. Something was not quite right and why did it always seem these men were watching him – or was it purely a coincidence?

As he settled down beneath the warm duvet, he found sleep was difficult; he couldn't take his mind off the black car and those men. And why did one always seem to ring a bell?

9

The Chase is on

Peter took breakfast early and went to reception to settle his bill. The amount was minimal: a couple of phone calls, no drinks from the mini bar in his room and everything else was paid for already by the tourist office. *Wow!* thought Peter. *I thought it was me who was on expenses!*

The receptionist offered him directions for the Arlberg. He was told to head out of Kitzbühel and follow the signs for Soll and Kufstein, which would take him onto the motorway leading either to Munich or Innsbruck.

'You follow direction Innsbruck and this motorway goes past Austria's third city and it is signposted Arlberg,' said the very delightful receptionist.

Having thanked her, Peter put his suitcase and laptop in the car boot and set off. The roads around Kitzbühel were quiet and he was soon heading in the direction of the motorway and not long afterwards, the sign for Innsbruck appeared. Peter carefully negotiated the slip road, watched in his mirror and joined a steady stream of traffic, all heading quite fast and some well in excess of the official speed limit. Peter was in no particular rush; he knew his journey would take around three hours so he planned a mid-morning stop for coffee en route.

He was surprised by how quickly the city of Innsbruck came and went: a great motorway skirting the university town with an airport just a stone's throw from the city. However, the closeness of the mountains made Peter wonder whether he would ever want to fly in during bad weather.

It was 11.00 a.m. and a well-signposted motorway rest area came into view. *Time for a coffee and a quick pop to the loo*, thought Peter. Once inside, the smell of hot chocolate drifted across and he decided on this rather than a coffee. After all, he had over indulged with three cups at breakfast.

Having completed his comfort stop, Peter allowed himself a few minutes to wander around the well-stocked shop and then made his way back to his car. As he carefully pulled out and re-joined the fast-moving motorway traffic, his attention was fixed on a black car – the black car he had seen in Kitzbühel.

'This is becoming too much of a coincidence,' said Peter to himself, trying to concentrate on not annoying other road users, but at the same time keeping one eye on the mirror and the black limousine, which was keeping its distance. 'I'll just cruise at a steady hundred and ten kilometres per hour and see what happens,' said Peter, again to himself.

The distances sped by, the black car remained a few hundred metres behind and Peter nearly missed the sign indicating the town of Landeck and the Arlberg Pass. He knew he had to keep going until he saw the sign for St Christoph and St Anton. If he missed this junction, he would be at the Arlberg Tunnel and would have gone too far.

The motorway entered an impressive tunnel, well-lit and obviously only recently finished. The speed limit was just 80 kph and Peter had quickly learned this represented 50 mph. There was no overtaking, so no chance of the black car gaining on him.

'Where is it?' Peter couldn't focus long enough in his mirror to spot the car and his full attention was needed for the road ahead. Suddenly, the junction road sign for St Christoph and St Anton came into view and as the motorway left the tunnel, Peter slowed down. He realised the road had been climbing during his time in the tunnel and there were traces of snow now on the road. Certainly, the slip road was snow-covered and slightly slippery.

Peter then joined an ordinary road, glanced in his mirror and there was no sign of the black limousine. He had been imagining things – or had he?

The snow-covered, single-carriageway road required all his attention. The road was by no means straight and he did not want to enter a bend too quickly and find himself sliding. Surprisingly, the road skirted both St Christoph and the main village of St Anton, so Peter promised himself a separate visit to see both.

The road had climbed and there was a sign indicating he had reached the summit so he carefully pulled over. *Must get a photo*, he thought to himself. One for the album, if not the newspaper, so he made sure his car was in the picture.

The road ahead forked, right for Lech and Zurs, which was where most of the cars were heading for. Peter was thankful for the other traffic on the road, as it meant that he didn't have to drive too quickly. He was also reassured by the fact that nobody else had bothered with snow chains, so it should be okay. What a view as the road snaked through tunnel after tunnel before finally emerging out onto a plateau, but his joy was short-lived; ahead was a police car and an obvious police check. Peter was one of the unfortunate cars pulled over. *Oh dear! What now?* he thought.

He wound down the window and an anorak-clad officer crouched down and politely asked him in fairly good English where he was going. Peter explained that he was a British journalist going to Lech and had an appointment at the tourist office. The officer asked Peter to get out of the car and produce his passport and driving licence. Having satisfied himself that the documents were in order, the officer pointed out that snow conditions could suddenly worsen at this altitude and a sudden fall of snow meant snow chains had to be fitted. 'I wish to see you have chains for the car,' he said.

Peter opened the boot and the officer looked inside and saw the chains.

'Very good. You know, we do find some British motorists attempting to drive here without chains. The fine is heavy and there is no excuse, but you are okay. If the sign on the approach road indicates snow chains, you must fit them before attempting the journey.'

Having thanked him, Peter got back into his car and carefully drove away. 'Just as well I took advice back in the UK and carried chains. A heavy fine would not look good on the expenses claim,' he chuckled to himself.

The tourist office was right in the centre of Lech and on the main street with parking immediately outside. Peter noted the twenty-minute-only parking restriction.

Inside, he found the front desk staff all spoke English and after a quick phone call, he was taken to a first-floor office to meet the director.

'Welcome, Mr Kingston. I received a phone call this morning from Herr Schaffer saying you had left Kitzbühel, so I congratulate you on your safe and quick journey.' The director, whom Peter guessed to be in his early fifties, then introduced himself with a business card indicating Herr Werner Fink.

'Is your car parked outside?' he enquired.

Peter said, 'Yes,' and Herr Fink told him that not even the tourist director could argue with parking regulations. 'Our police have to be very strict about parking otherwise our small village streets would quickly – how you say? – log up with cars.'

Peter politely pointed out the expression was 'jam up'.

To this, the director smiled and said, 'You English have some funny expressions. I thought jam was for putting on bread.'

Herr Fink then suggested they go and move Peter's car to the hotel and perhaps have something to eat. 'Or did you eat on your journey?' he asked.

Peter assured him he hadn't, as they walked to the car, and was suddenly feeling peckish.

The director went to get into the driver's seat. 'Oh, I forgot you English still drive on the wrong side of the road in your country. Perhaps being part of Europe should mean you should drive on the same side as we do?'

Peter wasn't sure if this was meant as a joke, but he kept his reply to himself and concentrated on the directions now being given. 'We drive a few hundred metres back in the direction you came and take the first road on the right,' said Herr Fink.

The Hotel Adler had five stars outside.

'I hope this will prove comfortable for you. It is usually occupied for some of the winter by the Royal Family from Denmark, but this year they will come to Lech at the end of January, so there is a room for you,' he said.

Peter was overwhelmed by the palatial front entrance and reception. He was expected and, obviously, the tourist director carried some clout. Immediately, the hotel manager (or was he the hotel director?) appeared, welcomed Peter and escorted them to an equally expensive-looking restaurant.

'If you give me your car keys, Mr Kingston, the porter will park your car in our underground parking area and arrange for your luggage to be taken to your room,' said the hotel manager.

A little later, Herr Fink suggested smoked trout. 'It is from our own local river,' he said. 'Tonight I have arranged a dinner for us at a mountain restaurant, which has house specialties. Tomorrow, you can eat here in your hotel, but we pride ourselves in Lech that wherever you eat, it is always good.'

The trout was washed down with an excellent white wine, slightly on the dry side, but despite usually preferring red, Peter had to agree it was a good wine to have with the trout. As they ate, Peter and Herr Fink discussed the purpose of Peter's visit, the type of articles he was writing and what he could write about Lech.

'I am sure you will wish to write about our royal visitors, but we do not wish to put off ordinary tourists. Of course, royalty is a little special, but we try and treat all guests in Lech as royalty,' said Herr Fink, smiling.

Peter realised Herr Fink had a better sense of humour than he had previously given him credit for.

Quickly, the meal was at an end and Herr Fink explained that he had to get back to his office for another meeting. 'In half an hour, a lady from my office will arrive and take you on a conducted tour of our village. She speaks good English, better than me I think, so you can ask her anything. We will see each other here at seven o'clock when I will collect you for our evening meal appointment on the mountain.'

With that, Herr Fink was gone and Peter made his way back out to reception.

'Ah, Mr Kingston,' said the manager. 'Your luggage is in your room; it is number one hundred and one and I hope you find everything to your satisfaction. You must inform us if you require anything. Now my receptionist will show you to your room.'

Peter thanked him and made his way up the elegant staircase to the first floor. His room was at the far end and as the receptionist opened the door, she explained the room gave excellent views across the village to the mountains. 'It is very quiet here,' she said.

Peter just had time to telephone his office and give details of the hotel in Lech where he could be contacted for the next two days. He asked the secretary to inform his editor that another article would be forthcoming before his departure.

As Peter was putting his toilet items in the bathroom, the telephone rang. The receptionist informed him that the lady from the tourist office was downstairs waiting for him. Peter quickly put on a jumper beneath his anorak, his warm winter walking boots and made his way to the entrance lobby. Waiting for him was a young lady in her early twenties with flowing, blonde hair coming from beneath a red and yellow ski hat.

'Good afternoon, Herr Kingston. I am Daniela and I will show you around our village. I see you are well-equipped against the cold and have good walking boots. That's fine. Shall we go?'

Through the front door and out into the narrow road, snow piled up at the sides. 'We can get four metres of snow here during the winter and our ski season is usually long, from early December until late April and sometimes into the first weekend of May. Some of the taxes that tourists pay as part of their bill goes towards snow-clearing, putting down grit and small stone chippings, and clearing the walkways for the people,' said Daniela.

In the distance, Peter heard the sound of bells and looming into view were two horse-drawn sleighs full of people.

'Many, many of our visitors like to take such a ride. The Netherlands people, the English and even the Germans from the north love the experience of a ride out from the village and into the tree-lined valleys.'

Peter asked Daniela where she had learned her good English.

'Thank you for the compliment, Herr Kingston. I learned mostly in the school and then in the tourism university. You see, it is a requirement of working in a tourist office here in Austria that you must speak at least one other language, so I learned English and Russian.'

Peter was amazed and remarked, 'Russian? Do you get many visitors from that country?'

Daniela said there was a growing tourist trade from countries which had once been part of the Soviet empire. Quickly changing the subject, she pointed out the small river running down the side of the main street. 'It comes from a large lake, which is full of forellen – I think you say trouts. We have as many trouts as you have sheeps!'

This made Peter laugh out loud and Daniela looked puzzled. 'Did I make – how you say? – a joke, Herr Kingston?'

Peter said, 'Please, call me Peter. May I call you Daniela? No, you didn't make a joke and I apologise for my rudeness. You see our English language is rather difficult and more than one trout does not have an "s" in the same way a flock of sheep is described the same as one sheep,' he said.

Daniela said she had found the English grammar more difficult to understand than Russian. 'You must always correct me, Peter. It will help with my learning.'

As they neared the bottom of the main street, Daniela pointed out the entrance to the large underground car park. 'This is why you do not see many visitors' cars in our village. We hide them away. Guests do not need a car; we provide a free ski-shuttle bus service from early morning until midnight. You just show the driver your lift pass,' explained Daniela. 'Which reminds me; next we go to the main lift station where I have arranged a lift pass for two days for you, Peter. Perhaps you will take a ride on our super new cable car and we will have a hot chocolate at the top station?'

To Peter, that sounded a great idea. However, he had never been in a cable car to such a height before, and glancing up at the mountain, he had a slight feeling of apprehension.

Peter's two-day ski pass was quickly handed over after Daniela had signed a paper. 'The tourist office must account for each free ticket we ask for. You see, the lift company is quite separate from our office, but we receive help for journalists who visit,' said Daniela.

Peter was surprised by how many people were getting into the cable car. Surely, there wasn't room for everyone and he asked just how many people could be transported each time.

'Oh, this new one takes a hundred and twenty people; you can see our older cable car alongside. That one transports only ninety people, but they go very frequently, every fifteen minutes in the busy season, so guests do not wait too long,' she explained.

As they boarded, bells started ringing, an attendant closed the doors and the cable car started to move, slowly at first but then more quickly. Peter was holding onto the side rail, although he couldn't move very far with so many people.

'I see you are a little concerned. It is quite safe, Peter. We have not lost a visitor yet!'

How reassuring, thought Peter as the cable car sped higher and higher and the mountain rock face seemed to be getting ever closer. *How will we get over that?* thought Peter. Then the cable car slowed and another one came into view going in the opposite direction.

'The halfway point,' Daniela said. 'The total ride is only six minutes.'

Suddenly, the cable car lurched slightly and swung. Peter's face must have turned white because now it was Daniela's turn to laugh.

'We are just going over the first pylon. Soon the top station will come into view. Most people are a little nervous on their first ride,' said Daniela. Peter explained it was the height the cable car was reaching. 'My previous experience was to a lower altitude,' he said with a smile.

Then it was over. They arrived very slowly into what seemed a specially built landing point, which the aluminium cable car fitted snuggly into. The doors opened and they were outside with skiers and their skis quickly heading for the exit door.

'We can see the ski slopes from the restaurant window. You can also look down on our village from here,' said Daniela.

Peter wasn't too sure about the latter idea; it seemed they had climbed many thousands of feet in just a short time.

Sitting in the restaurant, Daniela ordered two hot chocolates and told Peter he would get a press information pack from the tourist director that evening.

'I'm sorry you won't be there this evening, Daniela. I'm enjoying your company,' he said, hoping not to embarrass her.

'Oh, but I will be, Peter. The director has suggested I join you. He does not often invite me, so perhaps he regards you as very important,' she said.

Peter was delighted.

Once they had finished their drinks, Daniela showed Peter the views across the mountains and the many lifts, which served the high slopes above Lech. She also told him the resort was linked to Zürs, a small resort, which he would have driven through to get to Lech.

They boarded the next cable car back down to the village. Peter was so struck by the views that he had forgotten his apprehension until they went over the pylon. Again, the cable car swung and Daniela just smiled at him. At the bottom station, she suggested they walk back to Peter's hotel.

'I'm sure you'll want to shower and perhaps you have some work before the tourist director collects you this evening?'

Chatting about everything and nothing, but just making small talk, Peter nearly missed the black limousine parked outside another hotel. 'This is not funny,' he said to himself, but out loud.

Daniela turned and looked at him. 'Did you say something, Peter?'

'Oh, it's nothing really, except I keep seeing this same black car wherever I go. It's becoming too much of a coincidence,' he said, feeling that something was certainly not quite right.

'Peter, we have many such expensive-looking, black cars coming here to Lech. Look, it has a number and a NL from the Netherlands. I am sure you need not be concerned,' said Daniela.

It was nearly 4.00 p.m. what they reached the Hotel Adler and beginning to get dark. Daniela said she would see Peter at the mountain restaurant and with a quick handshake, she was heading back in the direction of the tourist office.

At reception, Peter asked for his key.

'There is a message for you, Mr Kingston; it was left here about an hour ago. The man did not give a name, just asked if you were staying here and which room,' said the receptionist.

Peter walked slowly up the staircase to his room. One inside, he put on the lights, closed the curtains, sat down on his bed and opened the plain, white envelope. The message was simple and to the point:

We know why you're here. We're watching your every move. You should watch your back carefully.

Peter was shocked. Suddenly the appeal of touring around Europe and writing travel articles had taken on a sinister meaning, but what could such a message mean? As far as he knew, he hadn't crossed anyone. Or perhaps he was being mistaken for somebody else. Perhaps a hot shower would clear his head.

10

Face to Face with the Enemy

Peter put a call through to England. He needed to talk to someone about his worries and Sue would be the best person. But she wasn't at the magazine and nor was she expected in tomorrow. Peter was told he should try her home number if he had it. Peter redialled, but the answer phone was on.

'Sue, it's Peter. Look I have a problem or what seems to be a potential problem. Can you get back to me later this evening, say after ten your time?'

There was nothing more he could do so he stripped off and ran a warm shower. He was just towelling himself dry when the phone rang. He rushed to pick it up.

'Sue?'

'Mr Kingston, this is the hotel reception. The tourist director will be a little late; he will collect you fifteen minutes later than he arranged.'

Peter thanked the receptionist and put down the phone, really disappointed, not because dinner would be late but because he needed to speak to Sue, and quickly.

It was nearly 7.30 p.m. when Herr Fink arrived, apologising for his lateness, which he said was unavoidable. They drove to the far end of the village and parked.

'Now we ride,' said Herr Fink. 'Not so high as you went this afternoon but to another part of our village called Hoch Lech. This means high,' explained Herr Fink.

Peter was surprised by the large collection of hotels, guesthouses and a small number of private homes. 'How do people get here to their hotels? Does all the luggage come up on this gondola link?' enquired Peter.

'No, I will show you. We have a clever underground system which transports luggage, food, drink and other items from the bottom station direct as required to each individual hotel,' said Herr Fink.

They got out of the gondola and walked a short distance to the nearest hotel where they were met by the owner. Herr Fink explained that he would like to show the underground transportation system, so they went down two levels and came out into a large room to what seemed like the luggage carousel normally found at an airport.

'Items have labels with codes placed on them at the bottom station. As they near this high part of our village, a computer sensor reads the labels and directs the items to each hotel's individual station, such as we are in now. Of course, in the summer, when we do not have snow on the roads, you can drive up to this part of the village quite easily. But in winter we prefer guests' cars and delivery vehicles to remain down,' said Herr Fink.

Peter was sufficiently impressed.

They went back up into the lift and to the lounge bar, where Herr Fink asked Peter what he would like to drink before dinner.

'A small beer please,' said Peter. He looked around the room and immediately his attention focused on the three men sitting near the open fire at the far end of the bar. The bearded man looked back and the two stared at each other. Peter could hardly believe what was again happening to him and Herr Fink caught the look.

'Is there something wrong, Mr Kingston? Do you know these people? You have a – how do you say? – very worried look on your face.'

Peter said he didn't know them, but seemed to keep meeting them. He explained about seeing them in Kitzbühel and how the black car appeared to have been following him, but he didn't mention the note at his hotel.

Herr Fink left the bar and went to reception. He was back within a few minutes. 'I have had a quick word with the manager and he will look at the guest list and inform me who these people are and when they booked. I am sure you have nothing to worry about Mr Kingston, so shall we go and enjoy our meal?'

Peter felt quite embarrassed to share his concerns with the tourist director. After all, he was here to write an article extolling the virtues of this lovely Austrian ski resort, not to become involved in something that was probably not directed at him anyway.

Their meal started with an excellent pâté served with slices of warm toast and washed down with a white wine produced in upper Austria. This was followed by what appeared to be a thick, green pea soup with pieces of bacon. Then they helped themselves to an extensive salad bar and the main dish was locally caught trout. The portion was so large that Peter jokingly asked Herr Fink if they fed the fish with a special food.

'Our trouts feed for most of the year on natural food in the river and our large lake. But hotels such as this one have their own large fish tanks and keep an ample supply of live trouts swimming until they are required by guests. Your fish was still alive thirty minutes ago, so you see it is really fresh,' said Herr Fink.

Peter thought better than to correct the tourist director about there being no 's' on the end of trout. Instead, he complimented Herr Fink on the choice of the main dish. The waiter then brought the dessert: a type of pancake filled with red currant jam, which was delicious. The cheese board that followed was so extensive that Peter had to apologise by saying, 'Well, just a very small slice of one of your local cheeses. I really have enjoyed an excellent meal and now I am completely full.'

Herr Fink suggested a digestive. 'It is schnapps produced by one of our own farmers and it does help to settle the meal,' he said and they retired to the lounge for the schnapps and a coffee. Herr Fink asked Peter if there were any questions he wanted to ask as the following day he had many meetings and might not have time to see him. 'I have prepared an information pack, which will inform you of our history and much about our village and some tourist statistics. I would also ask you again not to become too concerned with out royal visitors, but to explain what we have to offer the people from Great Britain when they come to Lech.'

Peter wanted to know what happened when severe winter weather closed the road to the village.

'Ah! That is a good question with an easy answer. It is seldom closed for more than a few hours. Our snow machines are very good and I think you will have seen the snow tunnels, which keep avalanches away. But we would not starve as there are adequate food stocks kept here in storage, which could supply guests for at least a month,' smiled Herr Fink.

As they left the lounge and made for the lobby and their coats, the manager approached Herr Fink and whispered a few words. Herr Fink nodded, shook hands and the manager asked Peter if he had enjoyed his meal.

'It was excellent, thank you very much. May I have a brochure so I can mention the hotel in my article?'

The manager produced one and thanked Peter in advance. With that, they walked the short distance across the snow-covered ground and got into the gondola.

'This works from six in the morning until half an hour after midnight,' explained Herr Fink. 'Mr Kingston, you were concerned about those men in the hotel. Now I can inform you they arrived this afternoon and asked our tourist office for accommodation for perhaps three nights. I also can tell you they are from Holland.'

Peter thanked Herr Fink but said he was still puzzled as to why he felt he knew them. 'When I see them I have a strange feeling, but I'm sure I'm worrying about nothing,' said Peter.

Herr Fink drove Peter back to his hotel and wished him a pleasant stay for the next few days. 'My assistant, Daniela, who you met this afternoon, is available in the morning to show you around our ski slopes, Mr Kingston.'

Peter said his goodbyes and went in to collect his room key. He was handed a message: *Please telephone Sue.* He quickly went to his room, threw his coat onto the bed and dialled England. Within seconds, Sue was on the other end.

'Peter, what's the matter? Your message frightened me. What have you got mixed up in?' enquired Sue.

Peter told her the whole story. For a few seconds, it went quiet at the other end.

'Peter, it's easy for me to say you're worrying about nothing because I know you and I know this sixth sense you have about something. Do be careful, Peter darling. When do you expect to leave and when will you be in Switzerland?'

Peter said he had another full day and another night and then he would be driving to Wengen. 'Have you managed to get some time off? Can you come for a few days, Sue? I miss and need you. I don't want to alarm you, but I've a really bad feeling about these men. There's something familiar about one of them, but I can't put my finger on it yet,' he told Sue.

'Yes, I've arranged some time off and will be at Zurich Airport the day after tomorrow on a Swiss Air flight, which arrives at a quarter past two. But you must telephone me tomorrow without fail, Peter. Promise?'

Peter promised. 'I'm being shown around the slopes tomorrow by an attractive young lady from the tourist office, so that will take my mind off things and keep me out of trouble.'

Sue was not amused. 'Peter Kingston, you really are the limit. Here am I worrying about what you're getting mixed up in and you're now worrying me about pretty young Austrian girls holding your hand on the ski slopes. I think the sooner I get out there the better.'

Peter told her not to worry. 'I'll be very good.'

Sue said that was what worried her. 'You're good in more ways than one, Peter Kingston. Just keep your mind on the reasons for being out there and save all your energies for when I arrive.'

'I promise, and I do love you, Sue, really. I can't wait for you to get out here. I'll sleep well thinking about the day after tomorrow and our phone call tomorrow evening. How about seven o'clock European time?'

Sue said it would be fine. 'I'm at the flat all day.'

They blew kisses down the phone to each other and then hung up.

Peter undressed, showered and climbed into bed. No need to worry, just concentrate on work and Sue's arrival in less than thirty-six hours. Wonderful!

11

The Penny Drops

But it did worry Peter and he had a troublesome night, mulling over and over in his mind where he could have seen the bearded man before. Why him? What had he possibly done to deserve threats and being followed by men thought to be from Holland?

In the morning, breakfast came and went, over which Peter made some notes on his laptop about the ski resort of Lech attracting the cream of Europe. But then, out on the slopes, everyone was the same. The lift pass cost the same, always supposing you were having to pay for it, the clothes certainly looked the same from a distance and whether you were royalty or plain old Joe Bloggs, you could take a tumble.

Daniela called for him at 9.15 a.m. and looked as radiant as she had the day before, but this time more colourful, dressed in her ski outfit: a matching red and white anorak and trousers with a red and yellow headband to keep her ears warm. She told him they would take in more sights from the village and after a mid-morning hot chocolate, she had arranged a sleigh ride up the valley to the trout lake.

'It is frozen over through the winter but there is an excellent restaurant called The Forellenhof. I know you had trout last night, so you can have a steak from our local reindeer if you prefer,' said Daniela.

They strolled down some narrow streets, keeping to the left of the river, and Daniela pointing out the various shops and other hotels.

But as they went to cross a small bridge leading towards the tourist office, they saw the same men coming in Peter's direction.

'Daniela, that's those men again I told you about.'

Daniela said they should just ignore them and walk on. 'Nothing ever happens here in Lech, Peter. I am sure they must be mistaking you for someone else.'

Near the bridge, the horse-drawn sleigh was waiting for them and soon the driver had covered them in warm blankets and the two horses, one a grey, the other jet black, set off at a brisk trot, the bells around their necks jangling loudly. As they left the village of Lech behind, Daniela pointed out various landmarks, including the various mountain peaks and the outline of a road. Daniela explained it came up from the other side of the mountains from a village called Wrath, but was seldom open in winter. 'It is quite hazardous to attempt to drive there in winter, so our snow-clearing vehicles make no attempt to open it from November through to the end of April,' she explained

Peter asked if this presented problems to the locals.

Daniela said it was only used by tourists in the summer and that people from Lech used the main link to the Arlberg Motorway in the winter.

Soon the frozen lake and the restaurant, Forellenhof, came into view. There were a few cars parked outside, but the restaurant was certainly not busy.

Daniela told the sleigh driver they would be about one and a half hours. 'He will wait as there are stables at the back of the building where the horses can be fed.

Inside, there was a blazing log fire and Daniela introduced Peter to the owner, Carl Stedmann, who explained that his family had lived for many generations in Lech and he would like to offer Peter a locally produced schnapps – a drink Peter was certainly gaining a fondness for.

Just outside the main restaurant was a huge fish tank and Peter was invited to select a trout.

'I'll leave the choice to you,' he said, not wishing to have identified his fish before consuming it.

As they ate, Daniela asked Peter about his journalistic career and how difficult a profession it was to get into in England.

'We have special colleges for journalists in the major cities, such as London, Southampton, Liverpool and Birmingham,' he explained.

Daniela told him that to enter the tourism industry in Austria it was usually necessary to have obtained a degree and she said she had spent four years at the University of Innsbruck.

As their lunch progressed, the black limousine pulled into the car park and the three men stood looking on. It was Daniela who spotted them first and told Peter. Both became slightly concerned but again Daniela said she could not imagine anything happening. So they climbed aboard the waiting sleigh with the driver soon covering them once again in the warm blankets. With bells dangling from the harnesses, the horses trotted back towards the resort.

Peter told Daniela he had to do some more writing before dinner, but as he was due to leave first thing in the morning and make his way to Switzerland, he wondered if she would be his guest to dinner. 'This time it's on me, but only if you have no prior engagements, no friend waiting for you?' enquired Peter.

Daniela said she never allowed her private life to interfere with work and she would be pleased to join him for dinner at his hotel, at 7.30 p.m. Peter readily agreed and they parted.

Back at the hotel and having collected his room key from reception, Peter made his way to his room to start writing. Inside, however, he soon realised that someone had been going through his things. Items were out of place; his laptop was still switched on but no programme was open. He looked in the wardrobe; nothing was missing but clothes were ruffled. Peter was about to ring down to reception but the phone rang in his room first. A deep foreign-sounding voice informed him that his interference would not be allowed and then hung up. Peter was alarmed – what was all this about? Surely whoever it was must be mistaking Peter for someone else? There was only one way to find out. So Peter then telephoned reception and asked where the call had come from.

'We have not received any incoming calls to your room, Mr Kingston. Perhaps another guest rang you using your internal room number,' the receptionist informed him.

Putting down the phone, Peter found it difficult to concentrate on the notes for his next article. What was going on? Why was this person ringing and following him? Peter, never usually one to be concerned, felt he was being mistaken for somebody else and was caught up in things that were getting slightly scary.

After trying to put his skiing thoughts down in readiness for his next article, Peter showered and tried to relax on his bed, casting his mind back to everything that had happened since he first spotted the men in Kitzbühel. Why did the bearded man remind him of someone?

He had been dozing for about an hour when suddenly he woke from a bad dream.

'I know where I've seen him before!' he said to himself. He was in the courtroom following the hit and run case. He must have had some connection to the escaped drugs baron.

Peter dressed and decided he wouldn't spoil the evening by telling Daniela his fears and how he had connected the men to something that had happened back in the UK. But, composing an email ready to send later that evening, Peter wrote: *DRUGS. I believe Nigel Ewell, the escaped prisoner, may have connections here in Austria. I am following a tentative lead. Some men in a black limousine with NL plates seem to be everywhere I go and keep staring at me!* He addressed it both to his editor and to Sue.

The meal with Daniela passed quickly, in a relaxed atmosphere, with both finding out just a little more of each other. Daniela said she wanted, for the time being, to be a career girl. Her ambition was to eventually become either deputy director of a tourist office or even head up a small ski resort tourist office herself. Peter said his work was the most important thing in his life at the present time but spoke of his girlfriend, Sue, and her career on a London fashion magazine, which Daniela thought was most glamorous.

All too soon, the evening was at an end and Daniela said the following day was a holiday for her; she would be spending it near Innsbruck with her parents. Peter said he planned to have an early start as he was driving across to Switzerland, but he promised to keep in touch and to ensure the Lech tourist office received a copy of his article as soon as it was printed.

After a small peck on the cheek and a polite handshake, Daniela was gone.

At reception, Peter explained he wanted to get his email message off and was given the WiFi link. He asked if it would work in his room. 'Of course,' said the receptionist. 'We have very good internet here this high in the Alps.' Peter also asked to settle his bill and was told that apart from the meal that evening, everything else was met by the tourist office. Great!

Back in his hotel room, Peter started his packing and decided to take a few things, including his laptop, down to the car. Using the lift direct to the basement underground car park, Peter went to open the driver's door and noticed the front tyre was flat.

'Blast!' he exclaimed, then opened the boot and pulled out the spare wheel, leaving his laptop for the time being in the spare wheel space. He turned to go to the front of the car when he noticed the rear tyre was also flat. That's the last thing he remembered for some hours!

12

In the Clutches of the Drug Gang

Peter not only came to with a splitting headache; he felt decidedly sick. He was conscious of movement, of being in a car travelling at speed through the darkness, but as he tried to move, the nozzle of a gun appeared roughly at the side of his face.

'You will be quiet and not attempt to move, Mr Kingston, you pig of a journalist spy. But you will pay for coming too close to us.'

To Peter, the foreign-sounding, rough voice left no doubt that he was in a fix; just how bad a fix or where he was being taken, he had no idea. The car sped on through the darkness and occasionally there were glimpses of street lamps or oncoming vehicles, but for the most part it was complete darkness.

Finally, they began to slow, the car swerving round many bends and coming to a halt.

'Out!' said the voice and Peter was pulled from the backseat, realising for the first time his hands were tightly bound. No sooner was he out in the fresh air than he was violently sick; he realised he had been drugged.

His captors pulled and dragged him towards an open door, pushed him inside and slammed the door. It took him some minutes to gather his thoughts and try and work out where he was. The room was bare and cold with just one chair. There were no windows and the floor was of rough, wooden planking. The dim light was barely enough, but Peter realised there was little or no chance of a quick escape.

It was at least an hour before he heard the bolt of the door being pulled back and into the room came two men, neither of whom he recognised. Peter, who had been sitting on the chair, was roughly yanked to his feet and one of the men, his breath smelling strongly of garlic, demanded in a foreign accent and poor English to know why Peter had been following them through Austria.

'But I haven't. I'm here simply to write travel articles for my newspaper,' he told them.

Without warning, he was slapped around the face, punched in the stomach and one of the men shouted, 'You lie! We saw you at the court building in England, where we have been and you have been; we know you are spying on us.'

Peter was gasping for breath, his face stinging from the slap, his stomach aching from the punch, which had winded him. He could go on denying it, but he realised denials would prove useless and probably only bring him another beating. He just remained silent.

'You are a journalist spy; you use your job as pretence for finding out our business; for this you will surely suffer,' and he was pushed across the room and bounced in a crumpled heap on the floor, stunned and winded again, and with his hands still tied it was difficult to get up.

The men left the room and Peter was horrified at his predicament. Nobody knew where he was; *he* didn't know where he was; he was certain that escape was a non-starter and any attempt would bring a severe beating at best and at worst . . . the likely outcome wasn't worth contemplating.

It seemed like hours and Peter was near bursting point for the toilet when the door swung open and he was grabbed by two men and led from the room. It was dark outside and apart from the torchlight from a third man waiting outside, there was little to see, although Peter realised he was being taken through woods. Frightened by an unknown outcome, Peter was definitely relieved to see the dim lights of a building appearing.

The door was opened, he was pushed inside and came face to face with the bearded man he had seen during his travels around the Alps.

'What are you doing here in the Alps? You are definitely spying on us. You must tell us what you know,' the man said in a threatening but foreign-sounding voice. 'You follow us, why? We have been watching you.'

Throughout, Peter had been left standing and he still urgently needed to go to the toilet. 'Look here, I have no idea what this is all about. I am a journalist simply here to write articles for my newspaper group about winter sports. It is correct I saw you at the court building back in the UK, but I have nothing to do with that case. Please may I use your toilet?'

'Shut up! I do not believe you and you must wait for the toilet until I decide what to do with you.' And with that, the bearded man left the room through a rear door. For Peter, it would have been easier to sit down as the longer he stood, the more urgent his toilet needs became. *I'll finish up wetting their floor and that will really make them unhappy*, thought Peter to himself, but the dry humour did little to cheer him up.

The bearded man returned. 'You will be allowed to use the toilet, you will also be provided with a drink and something to eat, but we still do not believe your story and cannot allow you your freedom,' he told Peter.

The men who had led Peter through the woods pulled him from the room once more, outside into the cold night air, and pushed and pulled him to another smaller building.

'You can go in and pee. But if you try anything, I have orders to shoot you,' one of the men said.

Peter asked for his hands to be freed. 'It will be difficult to go to the toilet with my hands tied,' he pleaded.

The man pulled a gun and told Peter that should he attempt an escape, he would be immediately shot. 'No one will hear the shots; we are many kilometres from any other people,' said the man gruffly. Peter also thought it better for the time being to do as he was told. He didn't know where he was and therefore there was little point in trying to make a run for it. He would just bide his time, discover more of where he was and wait for his chance, if one presented itself.

Feeling better from relieving himself, Peter came out of the evil-smelling bedroom, which was obviously used by everyone as a toilet, allowed his hands to be tied once more and was led back to his original prison, where the second man had provided a hot drink of thick, strong, black coffee and some strange-tasting bread with quite dry cheese.

'Make the most of this; it may be your last for a long time,' the man sniggered and then slammed the door.

What a predicament. What to do next? Peter was simply at a loss to understand why these men thought he was spying on them. *I'm an ordinary journalist trying to do my best and I get caught up in some international drugs business. What a story!* thought Peter but then realised he might not live to tell the tale.

13

Where is Peter?

Back at Peter's newspaper office, there were worried faces. No new article had been received since the first two and the editor knew this was not like his young, aspiring journalist. Something was amiss! But what? The group editor was in discussion with Bert Maynard. Bert said he would contact Peter's girlfriend at the fashion magazine in London to see if she had heard anything. But just at this moment, his secretary appeared looking anxious.

'This strange email has been received, sent by Peter from his last known hotel address at the Austrian ski resort of Lech.'

Bert read it, but before he could utter a word, his secretary pre-empted his thoughts by saying, 'I've telephoned the hotel. Peter's things are in his room and his car's in the hotel's underground car park with all four tyres flat. His laptop's inside the car boot,' she said.

Bert Maynard picked up the phone and called John Riddell at the regional office. He read out Peter's short message about drugs, the escaped prisoner and the fact he was following up a lead.

'I think Peter could have bitten off more than he can handle. I suggest we alert the local police as well as Kent Police and meanwhile, I'll see if Peter's girlfriend can shed any more light on this,' he said.

John Riddell sounded angry. 'I don't hold with young journalists doing their own thing in foreign countries without seeking permission or advice. I thought highly of Peter Kingston until now, but

I'm having mixed thoughts about whether sending him to simply write travel articles was the right thing to do. He is obviously too keen for his own good,' shouted John Riddell down the phone. 'Inform me immediately when you have any news, Bert.' And he slammed down the receiver.

Bert Maynard asked his secretary to try and get hold of Peter's girlfriend, Sue, at the London magazine.

'Sue speaking,' she said.

Bert Maynard was put through. 'This is Peter's editor, Bert Maynard. Have you heard from Peter?'

Sue said she had received a really strange message about drugs, escaped prisoners and following up leads.

'Yes, yes – we have too and we fear Peter may be in trouble. He's disappeared from his hotel without his clothes, his car is still there with four flat tyres and nobody seems to have seen him since last night,' said Bert.

Sue explained that she and Peter had spoken on the telephone the previous evening and he had expressed his concerns about being followed by strange men in a black car. 'We were due to meet up for the next part of his writing assignment at Wengen in Switzerland. He was going to send his latest article to you this morning then motor the three hours across to Bern and meet me at the airport. I was just about to leave for my flight,' said Sue in a rather distressed voice.

Bert told her they were alerting the local police in Lech and felt obliged to inform Kent Police just in case there was a connection with the escape from custody of the wanted Powder Man. He explained that Peter had done himself few favours by getting mixed up in something that he was not there to pursue.

Sue explained it was probably Peter's journalistic instincts taking over, but quickly agreed that he shouldn't have become involved.

After hanging up, Sue got onto her travel agent and asked if her tickets could be switched. 'I need to get to the western part of Austria and hire a car from whichever airport,' she explained. Her travel agent promised to phone her back within a few minutes. Sue sat in her office, perplexed. Just what had Peter gone and done? Was he all right? There were a hundred and one questions and Sue didn't have an answer to any of them.

The phone rang, jolting her from her thoughts. Her travel agent explained that if she got herself to Gatwick Airport within the hour, she would just be in time to check in for a flight to Friedrichshafen on the German-Austrian border. Her tickets would be waiting at the check-in desk and a rental car would be waiting for her.

Sue thanked him, rushed out with her overnight bag and hailed a taxi to take her to Waterloo and the Gatwick Express train.

Meanwhile, Bert Maynard had been having a discussion with the police chief at Bregenz, whose territory covered the mountain ski resort of Lech am Arlberg. He was assured that the local police were carrying out routine enquiries as there was no evidence of anything suspicious other than a car with four flat tyres.

'Perhaps your journalist has rented another car and forgotten his baggage,' said the police chief. But he did promise to telephone if there was any news.

Bert Maynard was not overly impressed. He pointed out Peter's laptop had been found in the car and he would not have left his hotel late at night, but he was told that Peter was simply a missing person enquiry. He hoped that the fears he expressed to Kent Police would produce a more positive outcome.

To others gathered at the police chief's office, Bert told them that all they could do was sit tight and hope that Peter would make contact soon. 'This is really out of character and I'm seriously worried Peter has got involved in something which has got out of control,' said Bert.

Word spread through the editorial office like wildfire. Peter was well liked and his colleagues shared their editor's concerns.

Meanwhile, after an uneventful check-in and flight, Sue's Austrian Airlines plane landed at Friedrichshafen Airport and Sue collected her Audi diesel, having completed the necessary paperwork. She was informed that the car had the obligatory vignette for Austrian motorways and was given a map showing the road to

Bregenz and then onward to the Arlberg Pass and the village of Lech. All cars in Austria were fitted with winter tyres by law from October to April.

Fortunately, the roads were not too busy with traffic and Sue was able to concentrate on driving on the 'wrong' side. Certainly, accompanying Peter on his journey to Austria before Christmas had helped acclimatise Sue to local conditions. *Was it only three weeks ago that we celebrated Christmas Day together in Altenmarkt?* thought Sue as she drove at 110 kph up the Arlberg Motorway. She had been warned to watch out for the slip road turning in the tunnel and nearly missed it as a large, 40-tonne lorry was immediately in front of her.

But once out of the tunnel and on a quiet ordinary road, she climbed higher and higher and came to a junction at the mountain resort of St Christoph where the signpost indicated a left turn for Lech. Fortunately, the roads had been cleared of snow and as the car was fitted with winter tyres, Sue had little difficulty in travelling. But she had time to marvel at the original brickwork of the snow tunnels, where once horse-drawn coaches must have travelled.

She quickly arrived in Lech and having found somewhere to park, she made her way to the tourist office, where she introduced herself and said she was searching for the English journalist, Peter Kingston.

It was some time before Daniela appeared and introduced herself. Daniela explained how Peter had spoken frequently about his 'friend' Sue.

'We are all very upset and anxious about Peter. Nobody has seen or heard of him and this sort of problem never happens in our peaceful village. The tourist director has been spending time with the local police, but I will explain more over a coffee. Please follow me to my office,' said Daniela.

Over a much-needed drink after her journey from the airport, Sue listened intently to Peter's concerns about the black limousine and the man he thought was following him.

'Our office and the police could find nothing out about these people as they were not registered at any of our resort hotels. The police say the car registration number was from the Netherlands – but then we have many – how do you say? – Dutch people here skiing,' said Daniela.

Sue decided to go to Peter's hotel and try and find more information and Daniela promised to contact Sue there if any news was received. She telephoned to the hotel to say Sue would be arriving in a few minutes, the rest Sue did not understand, although obviously the conversation was about Peter's disappearance.

At the hotel, Sue was taken to Peter's room, but his clothes and the remainder of his belongings did not shed any light on why he had suddenly gone. The receptionist showed Sue Peter's car in the underground car park and the four flat tyres. She was told the police had examined the car but found nothing, other than to say each tyre had been split with a sharp instrument, probably a knife, on the inside of each tyre.

The local chief of police had contacted the regional police headquarters as this certainly appeared to have criminal overtones. Not the sort of thing that happened in Lech, better known for welcoming royalty and other celebrities, and only perhaps the occasional bit of petty crime.

Sue was mystified and just did not know where to turn next.

Just at that moment, a policeman arrived and asked Sue to accompany him. 'My chief of police wishes to discuss something with you,' he said curtly, but with a hint of police politeness.

At the police station, Sue was shown into the chief inspector's office. He rose, saluted and then held his hand out. 'Please sit down, fräulein. I have some news.'

Sue's heart thumped. Had they found Peter?

'Fräulein, as we informed your journalist friend's office, we carried out a search of your friend's car and we discovered hidden in the boot of the car a laptop computer. Can you please identify it?'

Sue immediately recognised Peter's laptop. 'Yes, it is definitely Peter's.'

Do you know the password? Perhaps it will contain a clue if we can open the menu,' said the chief inspector. 'We can plug it in.'

Fortunately, Peter had confided in Sue and she typed in a name and some figures. The screen lit up and Sue logged in. Opening the folder marked *Travel Articles*, Sue scrolled through and found the last article Peter had written. It had not been sent, but there was a P.S., obviously meant for Peter's editor. It read:

I think Nigel Ewell, the Powder Man, is here in Austria and following me!

Sue asked if this could be sent to Peter's editor immediately and perhaps the police chief would also be interested.

He certainly was and immediately dialled through to the regional crime office.

14

A Prisoner

Peter still couldn't believe his predicament. He still had no idea where he was, but felt sure he was still in Austria. His only clue was what one of his captors had remarked about being miles from anywhere in a forest. *Okay, well if he could somehow escape, the forest would prove as difficult for his captors as it would for him. Just follow a downhill slope or better still a stream,* thought Peter. *But first, be prepared for a sudden opportunity.*

The metal door was opened by a man shining a strong torch. He was accompanied by a second man, who checked Peter's bound wrists and told him, 'You come with us.'

He was then roughly manhandled, pushed and shoved outside and led down a rough woodland path. Peter observed there was the glimmer of dawn above the tops of the pine trees. Was this going to be his final dawn? Peter was certainly petrified about the situation in which he found himself. This was surely not what travel writing should be about. Perhaps he would be better off stuck at court and council reporting after all.

They emerged from the trees onto a rough track where the black Mercedes was parked. The rear door was opened and Peter was roughly pushed inside. Not a word was spoken by his captors and the car moved off.

They joined a main road and the first landmark of note Peter noticed was a castle across a gorge with a river running between the road and the castle. Suddenly, the car swung off the road, over an iron bridge and began to climb. The road surface was icy but the car's wheels gripped as they climbed ever higher. Then, round a bend, the entrance to the castle loomed out of the grey dawn. Eerie!

As they crossed a rattling, metallic drawbridge, Peter could see the huge castle doors opening. There were dim lights, but not enough to be observed from outside. Once through the doors, they emerged into a large courtyard where the car stopped, doors were opened and Peter was pulled outside. A group of really rough and threatening men stood around. There was still no conversation between his captors and Peter was led across the courtyard and put inside a damp, dimly lit room where the only furniture was a rough and uncomfortable-looking chair. There was a small window but Peter needed to be on his tiptoes to see out. Anyway, the view was uninspiring: just the tops of trees and what appeared to be the side of a rocky mountain. The light outside was still that of a grey dawn, but a few flakes of snow were falling.

At that moment, the bearded man, who had earlier questioned Peter, came in, accompanied by two others. Peter stepped back, fearing the worst.

'You are to be questioned again later,' said the bearded man. 'Our boss is not convinced that your story about simply being a travel writer is truthful.'

'But it is!' shouted Peter.

'Be quiet! We know you are trying to find out what we do and where our boss operates from. We certainly cannot trust you enough to allow you to leave. We intend to find out how much you know and how much you have told other people.' And with that the bearded man left with his accomplices, leaving Peter once again pondering his fate.

Later, some thick, black coffee and a chunk of bread with hard, tasteless cheese was brought to Peter's room.

Well, at least they're not trying to kill me by starvation, thought Peter.

The dawn was finally here. The snow was falling more thickly and Peter's room was now quite cold. He tried sitting and leaning back against the wall but this was just as uncomfortable as standing. He had already ascertained that there was no escape through the window, which had metal bars across on the outside and there was a long drop of over 100 feet to the gorge and river below.

Peter was fairly sure that this castle was the headquarters of the Powder Man's drug operation. Surely there would be clues to lead the police to it. Or was there a legitimate cover, which kept police off the scent? Peter was determined to try and find out.

Outside, there was considerable commotion, which Peter could hear through the door. Was that the sound of a helicopter? It seemed right overhead. If only he could see out; there were certainly quite a few voices and some were raised. Peter could hear what sounded like a heated exchange, but individual words were difficult to piece together. He gave up trying to make any sense of the situation and suddenly felt very tired.

Much later, Peter was suddenly awakened from a fitful slumber, pulled from his cold, bare room and manhandled across the snow-covered courtyard. A helicopter stood in the centre. Back inside another part of the castle, Peter came face-to-face with the bearded man and another man with his back to him, glancing out of the window. The man turned and Peter, jaw dropping, came face-to-face with Nigel Ewell – the Powder Man!

Ewell glared at Peter. 'Why are you here? Why are you interested in what I am doing? Ever since we saw you in that British courtroom you've been showing an unhealthy interest in me and my men. Why?'

So many questions and obviously Nigel Ewell and his thugs didn't believe Peter was innocently involved in writing travel articles.

'Now look here, Mr Ewell,' said Peter. 'I am here in the Alps as a travel writer and – yes – I did see you in that courtroom because at the time I was a general reporter and your court appearance just happened to be on my watch. Since then I have been given the chance to do what I have always wanted to do and that is to write travel articles.'

'Silence!' yelled the Powder Man. 'You lie well, Peter Kingston, but this excuse of travel writing is just a cover. It is too much of a coincidence that you are here and you have been watching my operation. I cannot allow this situation to continue. You have cost me money, threatened my European operation and this I will not tolerate!'

'But it is not true,' shouted Peter and as he tried to continue defending his position, the Powder Man brought his fist crashing down on the desk.

'Shut up! Shut up!' he yelled. 'You are a newspaper spy and something must be done.'

Peter was roughly manhandled by two of the other men in the room. To his horror, he saw Nigel Ewell pull a handgun from his coat pocket.

'Blindfold him,' he yelled and as a dirty rag was tied around Peter's face. Thousands of thoughts rushed through his mind, including, *if only I'd stayed at home and enjoyed Christmas lunch with Mum and Dad.*

He was sweating profusely; it seemed just a horrible dream, but was this really the moment of death? There was a distant click, a sharp pain across the side of his head and then . . . nothing!

15

Forces Gather for the Search

Meanwhile, back in Lech, things were beginning to move quickly. A team coordinating the investigation of Peter's mysterious disappearance had been established; two police helicopters had arrived and caused quite a stir amongst winter sports holidaymakers. One had carried a team from the regional crime squad, a second carried two top British police from New Scotland Yard as well as a senior diplomat from the British Ambassador's office in Vienna. They had swiftly been flown into Innsbruck Airport on specially chartered private jets.

Sue was being rather side-lined, certainly kept out of the loop, and became increasingly frustrated. After all, it was her boyfriend; it was her who had alerted everyone to what Peter might have inadvertently stumbled upon. She tried to reason with whoever was prepared to listen. But at this point, to no avail. Obviously, something was happening; there were lots of discussions, phone calls in and out and lots of pointing at a map on the wall. Finally, the most senior of the Austrian police decided it was time to evaluate every shred of evidence and to include Sue in their understanding of the situation.

'Fräulein, we believe your friend, Peter Kingston, has been kidnapped because of what he might have stumbled across. It is possible that the drugs dealer wanted not only in your own country but also across Europe, including – yes – here in Austria, is behind this crime and we are extremely anxious about your friend. We

Forces Gather for the Search

must assume this drugs dealer – you call him the Powder Man – has some kind of drugs operation in this area of Austria, although up to this point in time my regional officers had no reason to believe such a drugs operation did exist.'

The phone rang.

'Yes, yes, I understand. Keep me informed,' said the senior Austrian officer, putting down the phone.

All eyes turned to him and after a few moments of frustrating silence, he announced, 'There has been some unauthorised helicopter activity near Bregenz. It is believed to be near an old castle, which was purchased some years ago by a Swiss businessman. But the local police say they have found an abandoned black Mercedes with Dutch registration numbers nearby. It may be nothing, but it is our best lead.'

Everyone looked at each other and then there was chatter from every direction.

Sue blurted out. 'Peter might be there. Can we not go rather than just sitting here? I feel so helpless.'

The senior Austrian policeman said, 'It is better we wait here until my local officers have some more information. It is an hour-long drive from here and it would not be ideal to use our helicopters as we might frighten off any criminals who may have been using the castle for illegal activity.'

Coffee and cake was brought in, but Sue did not feel at all hungry. The two British policemen were hurriedly in conversation with the diplomat. One asked if he could make a phone call to the UK and he was taken to another room to use a phone there. Mostly, people just stood around; there was some small talk but none of this helped Sue, who needed to see some action. She trembled at the thought that Peter could be held captive or even worse. No, she must not contemplate thoughts like that.

The British policeman came back into the room, spoke first to the senior Austrian officer and then to his colleague and the diplomat. Then the phone rang. All eyes turned to the desk as the senior officer answered. He listened then said, 'We will come immediately.'

'Fräulein, gentlemen, a helicopter was about to take off from the castle near Bregenz. Some men have been apprehended by my officers there. A car apparently left earlier and may have headed from Bregenz into Switzerland, but there are few details about the make, colour or indeed registration plate. We will leave immediately using the two helicopters, which will save a considerable amount of time compared with a road journey from here down the Arlberg Pass. We have alerted our Swiss colleagues but with few details to go on, they express some difficulty unless they stop every car on the autobahn from Bregenz towards Zurich,' he said.

Sue's pulse quickened. *Oh please, God, let Peter be safe*, she thought as everyone made their way out to the helicopters. The pilot had the engines started, the rotor blades began to turn and with Sue sitting behind the two British policemen and the British diplomat in the first helicopter with the senior Austrian policemen, they set off.

The cloud level was sufficiently high for the snow-covered peaks of the Arlberg mountains to be clearly visible. But it was down the Arlberg Pass they flew, the motorway clearly visible as well as the railway, which ran up the valley, but was set close into the mountain side, so that every so often it would disappear beneath tunnels, which protected it from rock-falls and avalanches.

Dusk was approaching and although the flight had barely taken twenty minutes, the lights of Bregenz came into view. Also, in a field on the outskirts of the town, were cars with blue flashing roof lights and figures marking out a landing area.

Once on the ground, they all alighted, with the senior Austrian policeman being approached and saluted by another officer. There was a conversation and the senior officer approached the two British policemen, the diplomat and Sue.

'There has been illegal activity at the castle that you can just see on the hillside. Fortunately, our local officers prevented a helicopter taking off and the pilot and two known criminals have been taken into custody. The helicopter was carrying some large cardboard boxes and they appear to contain sealed plastic bags of some sort of white powder. I have arranged for these to be analysed and the castle searched,' he said.

'But what about Peter? What's happened to Peter?' yelled Sue.

One of the British policemen tried to console her, but Sue pulled violently away.

'Have the men been questioned? Surely somebody knows if Peter had been held there,' said Sue, sobbing, her usual stubborn strength slowly ebbing from her body.

The senior Austrian officer (Herr Superintendent Strodel) told her that questioning was continuing, but it appeared the car which had sped off had been carrying the Powder Man and Peter Kingston, who may have been dead or just severely injured.

'Dead!' sobbed Sue. 'Oh no! He can't be! Perhaps it wasn't Peter!' she shouted.

An Austrian lady police officer (Frau Inspector Backerie) comforted Sue. 'Fräulein, you must not think the worst. Perhaps it was not your friend. We are working on getting more information as quickly as we can.'

More police arrived from Bregenz and the complete area around the castle had been sealed off. All traffic on local roads was being diverted and foreign drivers pulled over for questioning. The senior Austrian officer in charge of the police co-ordination was then called across to a fully equipped police command vehicle. When he emerged, he had some news.

'Swiss police have set up road blocks on all the major motorways between the Austrian border and Zurich, which is where the Swiss believe the car was probably heading. They may have a plane waiting, but the Swiss authorities will be checking every passenger trying to board scheduled flights out of Austria,' he said.

Poor Sue was distraught with anxiety and no nearer the truth of whether or not Peter had been held in the castle; no nearer to finding out if Peter was alive or dead.

It was decision time. Sue approached the British Met Police and also the British diplomat and asked, 'Is there no pressure you can bring to bear? Why don't they question the men they apprehended at the castle once more? Surely the men must know more than has been revealed so far?' Poor Sue was clutching at straws and did not fully understand how police procedures worked.

Once again, the Austrian chief police officer approached them and suggested it would be better for them to drive to police headquarters at Bregenz and see if any further clues had been gleaned by the specialist team questioning the three men.

Hope at last. *Well maybe*, thought Sue.

So they climbed into two police cars and sped off in the direction of Bregenz, a journey of less than ten minutes. Once they arrived, more coffee and Austrian biscuits had been provided, but Sue couldn't eat – she didn't want to. Oh what a mess and surely not of Peter's making. He had a journalist's nose for sniffing out a story, but he would never have knowingly put his life at risk – or would he?

An hour passed slowly by, then the Austrian officer came into the room.

'We finally have some news. The two criminals we have been questioning are squealing like chickens and offering information in exchange for a deal. We have promised nothing, but said we will consider their position if they tell us everything,' he said.

'We now know that a journalist you know as Peter Kingston has been kidnapped from the Lech ski resort and taken to the castle we saw earlier. They have told us he was questioned, beaten and they know a shot was fired by the criminal known as Nigel Ewell. They say the journalist collapsed on the floor and was carried out to a parked car, which sped off shortly afterwards.'

It went from bad to worse. One minute nothing, the next minute hope, only to be shattered by even more uncertainty. But then one of the British officers came across to speak to Sue and told her to clutch onto every shred of hope. 'Perhaps he has only been badly injured. If he were dead, they would have left his body behind at the castle,' he calmly said.

Sue was not convinced. If only she were at Peter's side now, treating his injuries, reassuring him. But she could not have known

Peter's plight. He had come to in some sort of vehicle, his eyes still blindfolded and his head aching as if hit by a sledgehammer. *Hit! That was it!* He then remembered the gun, a shot and a searing pain before . . . the rest was a blank.

16

A Swiss Intervention

After what seemed an age, the vehicle came to a halt. Peter could hear a heated conversation. Was that a woman's voice? His mind was playing tricks. Suddenly, rough hands were gripping his head and shoulders and he was being roughly manhandled and half dragged. He was thrown to the ground and he heard a door slam. The same rough hands pulled the blindfold from his face and the glare of lights was just too much. He had to shut his eyes and then open them again to adjust.

In front of him stood Nigel Ewell and his bearded accomplice. Alongside them was a distinguished, white-bearded man who looked to be in his mid- to late-sixties. Next to him was a woman who Peter judged to be in her mid-thirties. She was wearing a uniform, but what sort of uniform? It was certainly smart. But what was that insignia? A white cross on a red background. Surely, that's the Swiss emblem. What would a Swiss-uniformed woman be doing mixed up here with a criminal gang?

Peter's head was aching, really hurting. He tried to sit up but was roughly pushed backwards by the boot of Peter Ewell's henchman. He laughed but the lady screamed at him, 'You rotten swine! You are cruel maniacs!'

Nigel Ewell's henchman went to throw a fist in her direction but Ewell shouted, 'Enough! We have work to do and arrangements to make to get away. Fighting and throwing insults will get us nowhere now that the authorities are looking for us.'

Looking towards the woman, he said. 'Treat his injuries. Make use of your military training skills for battlefield injuries.'

The woman came forward, bent over Peter and looked at the wound on the side of his head. 'I need my medical bag; this really needs stitching,' she said, looking at Nigel Ewell.

'There is no time for stitching; just patch up his wound and we must make plans for our escape. If your father does not cooperate we will shoot him and you will still get us out of here,' yelled Nigel Ewell.

So that was it. The man and the woman were Nigel Ewell's bus-pass out of wherever they were holed up.

The woman came back with a bag and took out a bottle of liquid and some bandage. 'Hello,' she said, smiling. 'My name is Ursula and I am afraid this antiseptic will hurt a little, but your wound needs cleaning.'

She gently daubed some liquid on the side of Peter's forehead. It stung like mad. He gripped her hand and she smiled again. 'Sorry, but I did warn you.'

In a quiet voice, Peter asked who she was.

'Shh! Not now. I will explain when the opportunity arises.' Her English was impeccable with little or no accent.

Nigel Ewell came across. 'That will do! Enough!' he shouted, the lines on his face enhanced by his growing anger. 'Now we must get the other vehicle and make our way by back roads to our plane. Do they know we are coming?'

Nigel Ewell directed his question towards the distinguished gentleman. But before he could answer, Ursula said, 'I will phone again and tell them to be ready in one hour.'

Ursula left the room to make the call, leaving Peter sitting and wondering what would happen next. What could this woman tell Peter that she did not want Nigel Ewell to know she was informing him? How were she and her father mixed up with such a notorious international drugs dealer?

A little later, Ursula returned and told Nigel Ewell everything was arranged.

'I hope for your sake and that of your father you will not try and double cross me,' barked Ewell. 'The fate of other members of your family hang in the balance, Fräulein Ursula. You will do well to remember that.'

So that was it, thought Peter, reminding himself of what he had earlier decided. *The Powder man has a hold over this woman and members of her family.* If Peter could win her over this might be a way out. He then thought about the mention of a plane. A plane to where and was Peter likely to be on a flight or disposed of? After all, dead men tell no lies.

Nigel Ewell suddenly announced, 'We go! There is no more time to waste. Driving the back roads will avoid any checks on the autobahn and we must get to the airfield at Interlaken while it is still dark. Fräulein Ursula, you will drive, your father and Peter Kingston can sit in the back with my man to keep an eye on them. I shall accompany you in the front to ensure you follow the correct route and do not attract attention,' he added in a most emphatic way.

Peter tried to get to his feet but could not make it unaided. Ursula came across to assist him, but again Ewell screamed. 'Let the prying English journalist alone! He has caused me enough trouble already. If he is not fit to travel, we will dispose of him here and now!'

Slowly, with his head throbbing, legs like jelly, Peter managed somehow to get to his feet and stumbled across the room to the open door. A blast of icy air hit him. Snow was falling outside. A 4x4 vehicle with Swiss plates was parked near the rear door. Peter noticed the distinguished gentleman looked worried and haggard.

Peter was pushed in on the back seat and sat in the middle, between the gentleman and the bearded henchman. Ursula got in the front and Ewell sat in the passenger seat.

'Drive carefully. We don't want to attract attention nor do we wish for an accident. We will keep clear of the motorway and arrive at Interlaken Airfield in the way we normally arrive. It will be just like any other business trip.'

Dusk was falling, the snow had stopped, but it had taken nearly ninety minutes for the journey to Interlaken. Peter noticed that ordinary roads were not cleared of snow and ice to the high standard of motorways. *Cost, no doubt*, he thought.

The car skirted the main town of Interlaken. Peter remembered from his travel research that it comprised four small villages grouped under the name of Interlaken. The airfield had once been one of many Swiss military airfields and this one lay close to the village of Wilderswil, south of Interlaken.

At the journey's end, Ursula pulled off the main road onto an airfield access road and came to a halt in front of huge steel doors built into the side of the mountain. Everyone was ordered out of the car, a small door opened from the main steel doors and a dim light was visible. Nigel Ewell ordered everyone through quickly and the door was then slammed shut.

Peter saw a huge cavern, obviously once used by the military, which now housed an executive jet. There were lots of packing cases and several people rushing about.

Nigel Ewell went across to speak to one of them with his bearded henchman keeping a close watch on Peter. Ursula and her father were called over and a deep conversation then took place. Obviously Ursula was arguing about something. Her father gripped her arm as if to steady her as she appeared from this distance to be becoming angry with Nigel Ewell.

She returned and informed Peter, 'We will fly from here this evening. I have to log a flight route and our final destination, but it is to a place my father's jet flies to every few weeks, so it will not be a problem.'

Nigel Ewell ordered his henchman to tie Peter's hands together behind his back and then pushed, shoved and prodded him towards a small room set to one side of the cavern. Ursula's father followed and the two of them were locked inside the room.

Ursula's father introduced himself. 'My name is Rolf Hauser and Ursula is my daughter, my only child. My wife and Ursula's daughter, Heidi, are held close by, but I'm not sure exactly where. All I know is that if Ursula and I do not do as these criminals demand, then myself, Ursula, my wife and lovely granddaughter will all be killed.'

Peter was astonished. He briefly told Rolf Hauser his own tale of how he was being mistaken for someone sent to spy and reveal Nigel Ewell's drug-smuggling operation.

'Certainly, if I got the chance, I would immediately contact the authorities, but I don't believe there's a chance of getting such an opportunity,' said Peter. 'But how, if you are a legitimate Swiss businessman, did you become involved with such a notorious international criminal as Nigel Ewell?' Peter asked the grey-haired man.

'I have been importing lead crystal glass from Southern Ireland into Switzerland for a number of years. My business is registered; the police and Swiss customs know I operate from here with my private jet, which I purchased two years ago as it is more economical to fly than my previous heavier, slower plane. Ursula is a part-time member of the Swiss Military Air Force and knows this airfield well as it is used twice yearly for military exercises,' said Rolf Hauser.

'What sort of plane is that exactly out there?'

Rolf Hauser explained it was a Cessna Citation Excel, twin jet engine plane, capable of flying 2,400 miles on a full tank of fuel with six passengers and a full payload in the 80 cu hold. 'The lead crystal glass is carefully packed in large cases and with a cruising speed of up to four hundred and ninety miles, I can easily fly to Southern Ireland, load and be back the same day,' he said. 'Although Ursula flies the plane, I am a qualified navigator – something I also learned while I was in the Swiss Military – so we comply with Swiss flying rules.'

Peter interrupted. 'But how on earth did you become involved with Nigel Ewell? Why does he have a hold over your family?'

Rolf Hauser went pale and remained silent for a few minutes. 'My business was lacking financial capital as I had lost money on a badly judged investment. I met this man, Nigel Ewell, in Southern Ireland and he offered to fund my financial needs, short term. He said he would provide me with the backing if my plane could be used to import his goods into Switzerland without any questions. Like a fool, I agreed as I needed the money quickly and he assured me his business dealings were legitimate, but difficult to import into Switzerland. He said my glass importation business was well-established and the occasional small package concealed in one of the cases would not be spotted or questioned. I realised too late that it was a stupid move, but I badly needed the money and Ursula has the small girl, the apple of my wife's and my eye, so I agreed. It was only later I realised I was helping to import high-quality heroin and cocaine, by which time this horrible man, Nigel Ewell, threatened to give information to the Swiss authorities, which would have ruined me, closed my business and brought shame on my whole family. Now I am in so deep I must go along with everything he demands,' said Rolf Hauser.

Peter thought through the dilemma. So Ursula was an innocent party in the big scheme of things, but was trying to protect her father as well as her own young daughter and mother.

'We must try and work something out,' said Peter. 'Perhaps we will find a way to alert the authorities or even escape from Ewell,' said Peter hopefully.

But Rolf Hauser shook his head. 'I cannot put my family in danger. We must do everything demanded of us. I do not know where my wife or granddaughter are being held captive; I do not know how many criminals he has working for him in Switzerland who we do not see.'

At that moment, the door opened and Ursula appeared, followed by Nigel Ewell and the bearded henchman.

Ursula spoke. 'There is a problem. The snow is too deep on the runway and the authorities say we cannot fly out until tomorrow. There are no snow-clearing people available to help this evening and they will not start work with the special snow ploughs until six in the morning. There is nothing more I can do, although I did my best to persuade them our take-off would be okay,' she said.

Nigel Ewell's face was red with anger. 'This is an intolerable situation. Obviously by now they know about our castle in Austria and although we have not left any clues, they can trace the helicopter, speak to the pilot and although he did not fly me from here to Bregenz, he knows a little and may talk. If my plans are delayed or even put in jeopardy, you will all pay and your granddaughter and your wife, Herr Hauser, will not be seen again.'

Nigel Ewell and his bearded henchman stormed from the room and the door was slammed, leaving Ursula, her father and Peter alone in the room.

17

Hot on the Trail

Meanwhile, back at Police Headquarters in Bregenz, the chief of police, having taken advice from colleagues, was pretty certain that Nigel Ewell and others had escaped, taking Peter Kingston with them. But just where had they gone?

The pilot and two of the men about to board the helicopter were still being questioned, as the police felt they were still holding back on vital details. However, they were the best lead the Austrian police had and a full search of the castle had not revealed any clues, other than one small plastic bag of some form of drug now being analysed.

The British policemen and the diplomat had listened and announced they would wait at a local hotel until there was more news.

'I have spoken again with senior Swiss Police at Bern, our capital, and they have assured me all major airports, train stations and border crossings are being watched. They do have small roads that cross borders, but local police throughout Switzerland are on alert to watch for unusual activity. No helicopters will be allowed to take off with special clearance. It is going to be difficult, but everything that can be done is being done,' said the Austrian senior policeman.

Another officer came into the room and spoke quietly into the ear of his superior.

'Gentleman, the helicopter pilot is known to the Swiss police. It is not his plane and is not legally registered either in Switzerland or Austria. He claims he knows little and was hired through a third party to fly a businessman out of Austria. He says he was not informed of where the destination would be and would only be told once they had taken off. Of course we do not believe his story entirely and he will face prosecution and perhaps a long prison sentence when convicted. We hope continued questioning and pressure will help to loosen his memory,' said the senior officer. 'The other two men are from the Netherlands and are known to be involved in the drugs market in Holland. Their passport details were sent to the authorities in the Hague, and customs officers from there are, as we speak, flying down and will arrive during the night to assist us with our further questioning,' he said. 'I have asked for some refreshments to be brought in. It will be a long night but if you wish to move to the local hotel, I will arrange for you to be fully informed if there are further developments. It is all we can do at this stage.'

Meanwhile, over at Interlaken Airfield, Peter, Ursula, her father and the bearded henchman were closeted in the same room. Ursula had organised some coffee and open Swiss sandwiches and until that moment, Peter had not realised just how hungry he was. This was despite his head still aching and Ursula had explained that he had been ever so lucky as the bullet had grazed the side of his head, but it had left a fairly deep cut.

'It really should be stitched and if your head is jarred again, it will open and start bleeding,' she said.

Peter wanted to ask many questions about what was happening but with the bearded henchman sitting in the same room and trying to listen to their conversation, he decided to wait for his chance. This came about an hour later when Nigel Ewell came back into the room, accompanied by yet another one of his gang. He whispered into the ear of the bearded henchman and then all three left, with Ewell saying he was having to make alternative arrangements for their disappearance from Europe.

Peter asked Ursula and her father where they were flying to and what could be done by informing the authorities once they had landed.

Rolf Hauser said nothing should be done that would jeopardise the safety of his wife and granddaughter. Ursula said she knew that Nigel Ewell and his associates travelled on false Irish passports.

'I have heard this man, Nigel Ewell, using a broad Irish accent and also his forged passport is in the name of Patrick O'Rourke. I have always put this name on the paperwork, which I present here to the customs authorities at Interlaken, and it has never been questioned and the same has always applied in Ireland. I have had to go along with this because I have feared for my father's life, but I have never really wanted to be part of these illegal dealings,' she said and explained that they used Dublin as the airport and a car was always available. 'You see, my father has the Waterford lead crystal glass delivered in cases and the goods and paperwork have always been cleared by Irish customs. So we land and take some relaxing time while our return flight cargo is loaded. Nigel Ewell, or Patrick O'Rourke, does not always travel with us. Sometimes it is one of his associates and you saw him this evening. But my father is right, we should do nothing to jeopardise the safety of my little daughter and my mother.'

At that moment, Nigel Ewell came back into the small room followed by the other two gang members. 'It is time to sleep,' he said in his typical raised voice. 'We make an early start in the morning and my Irish contacts have everything in hand. Providing you do everything I say and make no attempt to alert authorities here in Switzerland or in Ireland, when we land I will arrange for your daughter and mother to be freed once I am on my boat heading away from the shores of Europe.' His voice was angry and his bloodshot eyes appeared to leap out of his face. 'If you fail to honour this, I will only have to make one call and you will never see them again.'

Ursula and her father held hands tightly. Peter remained tight-lipped, not wishing to receive any more blows or bruises to his already injured body and head. He thought to himself, *This is a bit different from sitting in the quiet and reasonable tranquillity of the newsroom. Perhaps travel writing's not all it's cracked up to be.*

Peter made himself as comfortable as possible on his chair against the wall. He was certainly not going to sleep very well. Ursula and her father sat to the other side of the small, bare room with the cold, granite walls, and the only heating came from their own bodies. The coffee and open sandwiches had helped, but now Peter needed to use the toilet. He asked Ursula if there were facilities and she explained they were in another area of the cavern. 'I will bang on the door and try to attract attention,' she said.

After a while, one of Nigel Ewell's henchman arrived and Peter explained he needed to use the toilet.

'Wait, I will see if this is possible,' said the man.

He returned after a few minutes, tied Peter's hands in front of him, slammed the door shut and turned the key. 'You come with me but if you try anything stupid, you will die!' he said in a loud voice.

Using the toilet with his hands tied was difficult, but the man had refused to untie them. *Oh well*, thought Peter. *My chance will come.*

He returned to the room where Ursula was still awake but her father was sleeping.

'The morning will come and providing the runway is cleared and there are no paperwork problems, we will be departing around six o'clock,' said Ursula. 'Our flight will be about two hours but I am still uncertain how they will explain you, Peter, on our flight manifesto to the authorities,' she continued.

Morning did arrive and Peter woke from a fitful dream. How could Nigel Ewell let any of them free knowing what they did? He had a bad feeling about things about to unfold and then the man himself came into the room with two of his drugs gang. Peter was grabbed, his hands still tied and he was dragged from the room.

Ursula shouted. 'Where are you taking him? I will not fly you out if you harm Peter.'

'Shut up!' yelled Nigel Ewell. 'You will do exactly as I say or your father dies right now,' he said, pulling a small hand gun from his overcoat pocket.

The door slammed with Ursula and her father on one side and Peter with Nigel Ewell and the gang members on the other.

As Peter was taken deeper into the cavern, the walls glistening with moisture from the meagre small electric lighting, two more men waited. He was gagged, his ropes tying his hands together checked and then to his horror, a syringe was produced. Sweat began to run down Peter's forehead and his growing fear turned to sheer panic. Was this the end? Was he about to be murdered and his body left to rot in the bowels of a Swiss mountain? Peter's sleeve was pulled up and the syringe stuck into his arm. Peter's head spun; he felt light-headed and was pulled towards a wooded crate. As he began to lapse into unconsciousness, he was manhandled into the crate, but he had no recollection of these final moments.

Back in the small room, Ursula and her father panicked, wondering what had happened to Peter, and then the door was unlocked. Nigel Ewell entered and said everything was prepared for their departure.

'The plane has been checked; it is now being manoeuvred out to the end of the runway, which has been cleared of snow. Fräulein Ursula, you must sign the paperwork with the authorities and I will accompany you. I am using my Irish passport, as will two of my colleagues. There will be no surprise on your part, no hint to the Swiss customs authorities, otherwise your parents and daughter will not live. Do I make myself clear?' said Nigel Ewell, his anger once again showing through in his raised voice, and the deep lines on his face really pronounced.

Ursula demanded to know what had happened to Peter.

'You are in no position to demand anything. You will do as I say, but at this stage this interfering English journalist still lives. That is all you need to know,' he said.

Ursula and Nigel Ewell presented themselves to the customs office. The Swiss official looked at Ursula, studied the Irish passport of Patrick O'Rourke and commented, 'So, another business flight, fräulein?'

'Yes. My father needs to order some more crystal glass. It is an expanding market for us here in Switzerland,' she said, forcing a smile.

Again, the customs official looked at Nigel Ewell and the passport of Patrick O'Rourke. 'And you, sir . . . Will you be returning to Switzerland or will you stay in Ireland after your flight?'

'I love everything here in Switzerland; it is a beautiful country. But now I have helped Herr Hauser to establish his business and give him further marketing opportunities, I must unfortunately now spend the coming months back in Ireland. I have other customers to look after,' he said.

The customs official appeared satisfied, pulled a stamp from the office desk and stamped the manifesto.

Ursula and Nigel Ewell walked across the snow-cleared runway to the waiting jet. The engines had been started by one of the plane's engineers. Once again, Ursula asked about Peter.

'None of your business. Now, fräulein, your father is on board, so are my colleagues. You will ask for take-off clearance and there will be no unnecessary words with air traffic control. You know the price to be paid if there is one false move.'

Ursula took her seat at the controls. Her father was already strapped in the co-pilot's seat. Putting on her headphones, Ursula spoke to the control tower. She slowly revved the engines and with the brakes fully applied, the plane began to vibrate. Suddenly, Ursula released the brakes and the jet began to move forward, quickly increasing its speed. The runway markers passed by faster and faster and then the plane rose, the wheels leaving the icy surface behind.

Take-off from Interlaken could be difficult in windy conditions with mountains all around, but Ursula was an expert pilot and the executive jet was quickly rising into the clear, early morning air, slowly turning in a north-westerly direction and under the direction of Swiss Air Traffic Control. But Ursula could not relax. Where was Peter? What fate had befallen him? Had he been killed or just left in that mountain cavern to be disposed of by Nigel Ewell's henchmen? So many questions and no answers.

Nigel Ewell sat with the bearded man and another one of his henchmen in the passenger accommodation. Two large cases and a crate were stacked at the rear of the plane. Nigel Ewell waited until the jet had reached its cleared cruising altitude and then, unfastening his seat belt, approached the cockpit.

'Remember, fräulein, no conversation with air traffic control other than the normal flight clearance. When we are approaching the Irish coast, I will give you further instructions.'

The radio crackled into life. The jet was leaving Swiss air space and French Air Traffic Control took over, confirming clearance across French air space at an altitude of 27,000 feet. The miles sped by and soon they were crossing the open sea with the French coast of Brittany to their east. Their route avoided any direct contact with British air space and before two hours were up, they were under the control of the Irish.

Nigel Ewell approached the cockpit area and holding the handgun to Ursula's father's head, said, 'Fräulein, do exactly as ordered or your father will be dead before we touch the ground.'

Once again, his bloodshot eyes stuck menacingly out. His aggressive behaviour led Ursula to believe that Nigel Ewell used his own drugs. *The Powder Man! How appropriate*, thought Ursula.

The plane's radio burst into life. Nigel Ewell pulled one of the headphones to his ear and listened in disbelief. Irish Air Traffic Control was saying their air space had become restricted and the plane was being re-routed to the Scottish mainland.

'Demand to know what the problem is,' ordered Ewell to Ursula.

Ursula spoke calmly to the Irish authorities and was informed there was a security alert across the Irish Republic and all air traffic was being re-routed.

18

A Police Breakthrough

Back in Bregenz, the police had a breakthrough. All night questioning of the pilot, the arrival of the Dutch police and further questioning of the two Dutchmen had led to information about an import business of Irish crystal glass into Switzerland, used as a cover for importing the heroin and cocaine.

The three men had asked for their co-operation to be considered when appearing in court. No such promise could be made by the Austrian authorities, who told the two Dutchmen that an application for their extradition to the Netherlands to face further criminal charges would be favourably considered.

Conversation had taken place between the Austrian police chief, his opposite number in Switzerland and also involving the two British officers from London. Sue had been informed but wanted to know if there had been any news of Peter. The short answer to this had been a firm no, but she was not to give up hope.

In the Swiss capital of Bern, things were moving quickly and records of all private jet flights between Switzerland and the Irish Republic were being checked on a computer. There it was! A company owned and operated by a Herr Hauser based at Interlaken came up on the screen. He frequently flew to Dublin and his business, importing Waterford crystal glass, seemed legitimate. But if what the men had told the Austrian authorities was true, how had a Swiss businessman with no criminal record become involved in the smuggling of drugs? Nothing made any sense. Herr Hauser was

A Police Breakthrough

a respected Swiss national and a highly regarded businessman.

Interlaken Police were contacted and they quickly called back confirming Herr Hauser had taken off earlier that morning in his private jet, piloted by his daughter. There were three Irish passengers on board, all businessmen from Dublin.

Warning bells were sounding.

The Bern authorities ordered Interlaken Police to visit Herr Hauser's home and speak to his family.

The British policemen had already spoken to London and the Metropolitan Police were contacting the Dublin Police. Government officials on both sides of the Irish Sea were holding urgent talks. If there was a connection between the Swiss businessman, the Irish passengers and drug running, the sooner it could be stopped the better.

A message came back from the Interlaken Police. They had discovered two Dutchmen at Herr Hauser's home and both men had been taken into custody as they couldn't offer a sensible explanation for their presence there, with the rest of the family seemingly away. However, a search of the house, including the nuclear shelter, which is a requirement of all modern Swiss homes, had revealed Herr Hauser's wife and granddaughter. At last a connection! So it became clear that Herr Hauser was involved in criminal activity and probably with the fugitive drugs man, Nigel Ewell.

The two British policemen made a call to London and immediately decided to fly on a charter plane to London. Metropolitan police had spoken to both the Irish and Scottish Police to exchange information.

Back in the air, Ursula and her father were being angrily shouted at by Nigel Ewell. He again demanded they land at Dublin but Ursula said Irish Air Traffic Control were firmly ordering the plane out of Irish air space and it was to be re-routed to Glasgow on the Scottish west coast.

'We will not land there. We must find an alternative!' yelled Ewell.

'But I don't know of an alternative and I'm now being talked into a landing pattern by the Scottish Air Traffic Control. I must obey them,' said Ursula.

'You will ignore them. Make some excuse and stay at this altitude. How high are we?'

Ursula explained they had already descended to 10,000 feet and were being told to maintain that height. One of Ewell's gang pulled a map from his coat and together with the other man and Ewell, studied a map of northwest Scotland.

Ursula then heard Ewell speaking of a boat. Perhaps that had been their plan: escape from Ireland on board a ship. Somehow she had to let the authorities know. But her mind was also on her mother, little daughter and also on Peter. Just what had happened to him?

Ewell approached the cockpit. 'You will land there,' he said, thrusting the map in front of Ursula.

She and her father looked at it. 'But what is it? I do not recognise any of this area,' said Ursula.

'There is a small airport near Oban. It is quiet and by the time they realise we have landed, I will have escaped,' said Ewell.

'This is crazy. I need instructions from a ground control tower. Is the runway long enough for this jet? In any case, I have air traffic control asking what my problem is and telling me that I must land at Glasgow,' she said.

'Negative! Do as I say or your father will die here and now,' said Ewell, pulling the handgun from his pocket.

'You are stupid! You fire that gun inside this plane and we will all die, including you,' said Ursula. 'Okay, I will try but I must fly over the airport first to see if it is suitable.'

Ewell nearly exploded with rage. 'You will land there. You will not fly over as I do not want to attract attention.'

'No!' shouted Ursula. 'You are acting like crazy. Planes like this just cannot land anywhere.'

Containing his anger no longer, Ewell aimed at the cockpit instruments and fired. The jet suddenly veered to one side, throwing Nigel Ewell and his two colleagues off their feet with a heavy thump to the ground. Ursula fought with the controls as the jet was now rapidly losing height. She tried to make contact with air traffic control to declare an emergency, but there was nothing . . . only the Scottish coast coming up to meet them quite quickly.

With her father's help, Ursula wrestled with the controls as the plane veered first to one side then the other, with the wooden cases and crate sliding and banging against the fuselage.

Groans were coming from the largest crate.

'What on earth could that be?' But Ursula was in no position to find out. They were now flying at less than 3,000 feet and although still over the sea, there were small islands dotted around, with much higher mountains on the mainland looming up ahead of them.

Ursula spotted the town of Oban. There was a large island just offshore, which she guessed must by the Isle of Mull, seen briefly on the map produced by Ewell. Speaking of Nigel Ewell, he was just getting to his feet, but still holding the handgun. Then Ursula saw the airport. The runway was dangerously short and there was no room for error.

Smoke was beginning to come from the instrument panel. A fire warning light was flashing. Ursula made a sudden decision to land, but to sweep round over the sea as there was only one obvious approach. *This would not be easy*, she thought.

She banked the jet and as she did so, Ewell and the other two once again crashed to the floor, but this time hitting their heads on the metal sides of the seats. The large crate and two smaller boxes broke free from the flimsy straps holding them and slid to the rear of the plane.

Ursula flew out over the inlet, which separated Oban from the Isle of Mull, and made ready her approach.

'Lower the landing gear please, father,' she said with a cool head.

Her father looked less than cool but pulled the necessary lever.

Nothing! Nigel Ewell's bullet had shot out most of the controls and there was no accurate reading of their height.

Ursula skilfully steadied the swaying jet towards Oban but then turned slightly to the north for a once-only approach to a runway that looked far too short. There were small houses on a hill, which was fortunately not too high, then an iron bridge with some sort of river flowing beneath. Smoke in the cockpit was getting thicker and breathing more difficult. Ursula pulled back on the controls and attempted to slow the air speed of the jet without it stalling. Suddenly, the runway was ahead. Several people appeared from the control tower, waving their arms, obviously warning them off.

Too late! Ursula had made a decision and told her father to prepare for a crash landing. 'To hell with Nigel Ewell and his gang! With a bit of luck, a bumpy landing will be the very least they deserve.'

The jet hit the concrete runway with a resounding crash and tearing of metal. Ursula and her father were thrown forward and hit their heads, knocking them unconscious. Nigel Ewell and the other two men were thrown against the metal seat frames but had already been knocked unconscious.

The jet was still tearing along the runway and sparks were coming from beneath. One wing had come into contact with the ground and the jet was beginning to slew round and head side-on for the rocks to one side of the field. The people from the control tower stood in amazement as the plane began to break up. Flames were now coming from the fuselage. One of them rushed into a building and called the emergency services. The airport itself was only equipped with limited facilities and other people were running carrying portable fire extinguishers. One side of the plane where fuel tanks had ruptured was enveloped in flames.

19

The Highlands

Sue had asked the two British policemen if she could fly back with them as it was obvious the plane carrying the Powder Man had headed out of Switzerland and was going to be landing in the Irish Republic, where hopefully Irish Police would apprehend all those on board. A quick phone call to London and permission was obtained for Sue to fly back with them. The Austrian chief of police provided them with a car and police driver to take them to the airport at Friedrichshafen, just across the border into Germany from Austria. The plane they had chartered for the flight was being made ready.

Once in the air, the pilot relayed a message he had received to say the Swiss flight had been diverted from the Irish Republic and re-routed to the Scottish airport of Glasgow.

'We must also head straight there, Captain. Ask for permission for our flight plan to be changed to fly over London and head north to Glasgow.'

Permission was given as the pilot explained to the authorities that theirs was a private jet on police business. Half an hour later, the captain relayed a further message: 'The Swiss jet is ignoring instructions to land at Glasgow and appears to have lost altitude without permission. It's heading further up the northwest coast. But they say there are no suitable airfields.'

Sue looked extremely worried. All sorts of thoughts were racing through her mind, including what if Peter was already dead, left behind somewhere in Switzerland? But she had to know.

They flew on and the pilot assured the British policemen that there was sufficient fuel for the longer flight, which would add about an hour to their flying time. Half an hour later, a further message came through, this time even more worrying. A mystery jet had attempted to land at a small airfield near Oban, which was totally unsuitable for such a jet plane. It had crash-landed without any landing gear and was now on fire. Emergency services were rushing to the scene.

Sue's heart beat quicker and quicker, and she let out a small scream. 'Perhaps they're all injured or even dead,' she said.

The British policemen tried to calm her. No hysterics at this stage could alter things. They then asked the pilot to see if a helicopter could be made available to fly them to Oban. A message came back that a police helicopter would be waiting at Glasgow Airport; they had been given priority to land. They were also told that fire services were now at the scene of the crash.

It seemed an age before they landed and then transferred to the police helicopter. The two police officers were now speaking to their Scottish counterparts and some of the information was relayed to Sue. It appeared a number of people had been pulled from the plane; three were seriously hurt and two more were dead. Most of the plane had been destroyed, but the tail section of fuselage had escaped the worst of the fire damage and was being examined.

It would take them only twenty minutes to reach Oban Airfield. From the air, the charred remains of the executive jet could be clearly seen. There were emergency vehicles everywhere and people rushing around on the ground.

The helicopter landed near the main terminal buildings and airfield officials asked them to go into the building where a senior police officer was waiting to brief them.

'The lady pilot and a middle-aged gentleman in the cockpit have been taken to hospital, unconscious. They have superficial burns thanks to the quick work of airfield workers. They may have other injuries and are being assessed at Oban Hospital,' he said. 'One other man from the main fuselage area was also pulled out but he has more extensive burns. Two others were found and unfortunately are dead,' said the Scottish police officer. 'In the rear section of the plane there were some packing cases and a large crate. We have just examined this large crate and were shocked to find an unconscious man, bound and gagged inside. He seems to have a head wound, but the solidly constructed wooden crate saved him from the flames. The wood may have been pre-treated as the flames had not burned through to the interior packing material surrounding the man. He has had a lucky escape. Now he is in an ambulance awaiting transportation to hospital. Some of my officers are there to see if he regains consciousness before being taken to Oban for further assessment. Our facilities at Oban are good as it is a district general hospital; we deal with serious cases, which cannot be dealt with on the outer Scottish islands,' said the officer.

Sue begged to be allowed to see the man. 'Please!' she pleaded. 'It might be Peter.'

The Scottish police and the two officers from London went to one side and held a quiet conversation. Eventually, it was agreed that they would take a quick visit to the ambulance, providing the medics were in agreement.

'Please be prepared for any disappointment. We have no reason to believe this is the young man you are hoping for,' he said in a typical, policeman-like manner.

Accompanied by the Scottish officer and two policemen from London, Sue walked towards the ambulance where paramedics were treating the injured man. After a brief discussion with the policemen, one of the ambulance crew led Sue inside the vehicle.

'The man's unconscious and has a very nasty head wound. He could have other injuries as there are quite a few bruise marks to his body,' he told Sue.

Sue waited with baited breath as a sheet was pulled back from the upper part of his body. She let out a scream. 'It's Peter! This is my Peter! You can't let him die! Can I come to the hospital with you?' she begged.

The ambulance's radio crackled a message informing them that they should get the injured man to Oban General as quickly as possible, as a trauma team was standing by.

Sue sat in the back of the ambulance with one of the paramedics as the vehicle sped off with its siren sounding. Peter's face was white apart from a nasty, deep head wound, which was still oozing blood. There was little or no sign of life, although the machines to which he was wired showed a weak pulse and equally weak blood pressure.

'He is very, very ill, but I'm sure the hospital consultants will do everything possible,' said the paramedic. 'My colleague and I have told the hospital we believe some type of lethal drug has been administered and this may have put him in this deep coma. The readings we are getting are very low and we are seriously concerned. But he is alive and there is hope,' he added.

Traffic through the centre of the busy, west-coast fishing port of Oban pulled to the side as the ambulance with a police escort sped closer and closer to the hospital on the far side of the town and port. At A&E, a team of doctors and nurses were waiting to take over and the ambulance trolley was wheeled through automatic doors. Sue was told to wait in the relatives' room, but she would be kept fully informed of any developments.

Toxicology tests revealed that Peter had been given a drug that could have killed him, although its exact nature was not immediately known. As it was, his life hung in the balance and the next twenty-four hours would be the critical period. Meanwhile, a surgeon had examined Peter's bullet wound to the skull then cleaned it out and stitched the gaping wound. X-rays showed numerous bruises but no sign of broken bones.

'Your friend will remain in pain for some days, but first we have to get him through this critical twenty-four hours. If we knew what type of drug he was given, it is possible we could administer an antidote,' said the senior doctor. 'It will be touch and go and a question of whether he is strong enough to fight the drug himself until we can find the antidote,' he said.

The hospital made arrangements for Sue to have a room near to Peter's private room. Both the Metropolitan Police and Scottish

Police were keen to speak to Peter once he woke up. Other police officers were waiting to question the lady pilot and the middle-aged man. Investigations were continuing to try and identify the others killed in the plane crash. Interpol had been contacted and fingerprints had been taken in an attempt to speed up identification. Sue was warned it might be several days before Peter was able to talk or even able to be interviewed, always supposing he could recover from whichever drug had been administered. They would be pleased to allow her to stay at the hospital and sit by his bedside, but only when doctors were not carrying out treatment.

In another part of the hospital, Ursula and her father had both regained consciousness and had been X-rayed to see what, if any, other internal injuries they might have. Fortunately, both had escaped serious injury, although Ursula's father had suffered a cracked collar bone. Their burns could be easily treated, but would be painful.

Scottish Police were questioning them. Both had been cautioned, but said they would cooperate and give full details.

Ursula asked about the other passengers and was told two were dead and a third was injured with very serious burns and a head injury.

'We are concerned about the man found in the wooden crate. He has now been identified and his young lady friend is with him, but he remains in a deep coma,' said the policeman. 'What do you know about this young man? Why was he in the wooden crate?'

Ursula was shocked. *Could it be Peter? So that was what the groans were*, she thought to herself. She told the police officers everything: how her father was being blackmailed and how her mother and daughter were being held captive, how the drugs criminal had threatened to kill them if she and her father didn't do as they were told.

'Your daughter and mother are safe. The Swiss Police contacted the British authorities and they told us. So that's no longer a concern for you,' said the Scottish officer.

Ursula could have fainted with relief. 'Did you hear that, father?

Mother and Heidi are both okay. The Swiss Police have found them safe and well.'

Herr Hauser breathed a deep sigh of relief. He knew he was in trouble over the involvement of drugs in the importation business, but that was nothing now he knew his wife and little granddaughter were okay.

Another police officer entered the room and they left together. A nurse remained by the two beds, just a simple screen separating the beds. Because they had been identified as father and daughter and were foreigners in a foreign country, hospital authorities in consultation with the Scottish Police had agreed it was best to keep them close together. The nurse had been instructed to administer further treatment to the burns once the police had left.

In another part of the hospital, the most senior Scottish chief inspector was talking to the two Metropolitan police officers. They had also been speaking to HM Customs and Immigration. All were awaiting identification of the two bodies pulled from the plane's wreckage. Just then, a doctor came along and said there was an important phone call from a newspaper editor at Peter's office.

'He thinks he may know the identity of one of the men,' he told the police.

One of the Metropolitan officers went to take the phone call.

'Yes, Peter Kingston . . . Oh, the missing journalist and he works for your newspaper,' said the officer. 'So what is your name, sir? And what was one of your journalists doing involved in an international drug-smuggling operation?'

Bert Maynard gave the full story. 'No, Peter Kingston had been in Austria doing travel articles. No, he was still not sure how he had become involved, but be believed the escaped drugs criminal, better known as the Powder Man, was in Austria. Somehow they must have met up and they may have thought Peter Kingston was there to write a story and reveal their true identity,' speculated Bert Maynard. 'How is he? Can I send one of our senior staff up to interview him? This will make a great story!'

'Definitely not,' said the police officer with some authority to his voice. 'This young man is seriously ill, in a coma, and has a bullet wound to his head, which required stitching. It will be several days, if he regains consciousness, before I will allow you to speak with him,' said the police officer.

Bert Maynard thanked him and said he would call the hospital again the following day for a progress report.

Later that evening, identification came through on the two dead bodies. One was definitely Nigel Ewell; the other was from a South American country and was wanted worldwide for his involvement in the smuggling of drugs. News not only spread quickly through the hospital but had somehow reached the media. Reporters and TV crews had started to arrive at the hospital. Phones were constantly ringing.

'We need a full-time team just keep these news hounds at bay,' said the hospital's chief executive, calling the firm that normally handled press and PR matters. 'Get a full team up here from Glasgow as quickly as possible. These news hounds are disturbing the normal running of this hospital.'

20

The Final Chapter

It was two days later when Peter Kingston awoke from his deep coma. His head ached, his body hurt, but surely he was dreaming. A young lady at his bedside looked just like the Sue he knew.

'Oh, Peter! How wonderful! You're awake, my darling. You had us all so very worried,' but before she could say more, a nurse and a doctor appeared.

'Now, young lady, there will be plenty of time for you both to get re-acquainted later. Medical matters take precedence over matters of the heart here, so please go and get yourself a coffee. At least you can relax knowing your boyfriend's over the worst. But it will be many days yet,' said the doctor.

As Sue left the private room, a consultant and a team of young doctors in hot pursuit swept down the corridor into Peter's room. Peter himself was in a daze. Where was he? What was Sue doing? Why did he just want to sleep and why all the pain?

In the main waiting area and also drinking coffee were the two London police officers. They hadn't heard the news that the young man was out of his coma. Both jumped to their feet and started to go down the corridor as the medical team swept by.

'There's no rush,' Sue said to them 'They won't let you speak to Peter yet until they have done more checks. I couldn't stand Peter having a relapse.'

The officers conferred and went off to find a phone. London should be fully briefed immediately. But certainly it had been tremendous news that Nigel Ewell and his drugs operation would no longer be of concern.

'Our time here in Scotland will be quite limited once we've interviewed this Peter Kingston. Sounds as though his journalistic nose for sniffing out a story got him into serious hot water and he's lucky to be alive,' said one of the officers.

A big TV screen on the wall of the hospital's waiting room had a breaking news story flashing on the screen.

'Notorious drugs baron killed in Scottish air crash. Mystery man found in wooden crate in hospital on danger list.'

A news presenter appeared, outlining the story of how an executive jet crash-landed without landing gear at the tiny airfield north of Oban. 'Much of the plane, which had broken into three sections, has been destroyed by fire. The pilot, identified as a Swiss woman, and a middle-aged gentleman, both in the cockpit, have survived with burns and other non-life-threatening injuries, while a notorious drugs baron known as the Powder Man, who had escaped from custody while being transferred from court to Isle of Wight Prison before Christmas, has died in the flames. Mystery surrounds the man, described as being in his late-twenties, found in a wooden crate at the rear of the plane's fuselage. The position of the wooden crate and its construction had probably contributed to the man's survival. There has been a second casualty, also believed to be part of a drugs gang. Police and specialist drugs officers are at Oban Hospital waiting to interview survivors.'

'Oh well!' said one of the London police officers. 'For once, the BBC's got the facts of its story correct.'

Back at Peter's newspaper office, John Riddell and Bert Maynard had been in conversation about Peter.

'This story makes front page, especially now we know Peter's safe, although still quite ill. It appears from what I've gathered from the senior police officer in charge that Peter has been a real victim and is lucky to be alive. Perhaps I misjudged him, although I still feel he was pursuing a story that he was not in Europe to do. However, it shows he has the capability of showing that once a journalist, always a journalist,' said Bert Maynard.

That afternoon, in the evening edition, Peter's face was splashed over the front page with the headline, *Lucky to be Alive!* The article gave details of how the police believed that Peter Kingston, a top journalist on this newspaper, had discovered the whereabouts of Nigel Ewell – better known as the Powder Man – but had unfortunately been kidnapped. He had been shot for his involvement but surgeons in Scotland had said there would be no lasting damage from the head wound.

But the story was incomplete. Police were still being tight-lipped about the circumstances, except to say the private jet, which had crashed in the north west of Scotland, had been flown by a Swiss military woman pilot. It suggested she had played a vital role in Peter's rescue.

Authorities in the Irish Republic, acting on advice from London, had refused permission for the jet to land at Dublin and had diverted it to Glasgow. Just why the plane had then dropped in altitude and had been flown further up the west coast towards Oban was still unclear.

Peter's parents couldn't believe what they were reading. They had been completely unaware of what had been happening.

'I didn't want him to go chasing all over Europe in the first place,' said Peter's mother. 'If he had come here for Christmas, none of these dreadful things would have happened. Oh, my poor Peter,' she wailed.

His father just looked on. Any comment he wanted to make wouldn't help at this stage, but he was happy to know his son was safe. Peter's mother wanted to fly to Scotland immediately but her husband forcefully intervened. 'Now look here, there will be plenty of time for reunions once Peter has recovered. For the time being he is in the safe and capable hands of experts at a Scottish hospital. I am sure we can get daily updates, and when the time comes we can be together with Peter again. I am sure his newspaper editor will keep us fully informed,' he said.

The Final Chapter

The following morning at Oban Hospital, Sue was once again allowed at Peter's bedside. He was obviously still very unwell and just wanted to sleep, but a senior doctor assured her that he was over the worst.

'We're keeping him sedated in view of the bullet to his head and the other extensive injuries. But nothing's broken and he'll mend. We're still awaiting the results of his blood tests to determine what drug was administered to him. It's not clear whether it was supposed to kill or just sedate him,' said the doctor to an alarmed Sue.

'But he will get better? He must get better. I want to marry him. Oh, Peter darling, wake up and let me see you smile,' Sue pleaded.

The embarrassed doctor left the room and spoke to a nurse who came in to comfort Sue. 'I'll get you a cup of tea in a minute. Do not worry yourself. Your young man is in very capable hands and he will recover. I know the consultant and doctors yesterday discussed transferring him by helicopter to Glasgow, but obviously he is no longer in a critical condition, so he remains here with us,' said the nurse.

At that moment, Peter stirred from a fitful slumber. There she was again; could it really be the love of his life, Sue?

'Peter, darling, I love you,' said Sue with tears streaming down her cheeks. 'What a terrible time you've had. Just get better for me,' she said.

Could he be dreaming? Where was he? What had happened? He had had such awful dreams. He vaguely remembered being beaten then a syringe being stuck into his arm and then nothing. His head and body ached and he had a headache.

'Sue, is that really you? Where am I? Why do I hurt so much?' Peter wanted to ask more but he felt so sleepy. Why did he just want to sleep?

The nurse called the doctor, who said Sue should allow Peter some rest.

'He is slowly coming out of his coma. I don't think he fully understands what has happened or where he is. A few more hours of sleep will certainly help and you can see him again later today,' said the doctor, trying to smile a little comfort in Sue's direction.

Meanwhile, the two British police officers were being recalled to London. The police commander back in London had said further questioning should be left to the Scottish officers at this stage. HM Customs were making their own enquiries, but in view of the fact that Nigel Ewell was now dead, the case was closed.

Later that day, Sue was again allowed into Peter's private room. He was now awake but still in pain.

'Oh, Peter, I do love you. Can you understand me?' asked Sue.

'Sue, is it really you? The doctor says I'm in a Scottish hospital but how did I get here? I was in Switzerland when I last remember anything.'

Sue outlined everything she knew to Peter. She told him he had been discovered in a large wooden crate, which had probably saved his life. Peter suddenly had a flashback to Ursula, but what had happened? He knew nothing of the plane crash. So was she okay?

Sue said the lady pilot and a middle-aged man, whom police had now discovered was her father, were in another part of the hospital being treated for injuries and burns, which were not life-threatening.

'She may well have saved your life. She didn't know you were in the wooden case, but had intervened in Switzerland when Nigel Ewell threatened to kill you,' said Sue. 'You may owe her a great deal, Peter,' she said.

There was still so much Peter wanted to know but again he was feeling tired. When would he feel himself again?

The doctor appeared. 'How are you feeling, Peter?' he asked.

'Tired and still not understanding exactly what has happened, doctor,' said Peter.

The doctor told Peter that was understandable; especially in view of the drugs he had been given. 'Fortunately, results that have just come through show there will be no lasting damage. We now do not believe the drug was intended to kill you, just to keep you sedated. However, too much was probably administered, which is part of the reason for you feeling so awful. It will pass and now we know, we can give you medication that will clear it out of your body quite quickly. But I'm afraid it will be several more days of complete hospital rest.' Looking at Sue, the doctor smiled at Peter and said, 'And no excitement either!'

Swiss diplomats had flown up from London to interview Ursula and her father. They told both of them there would be a criminal investigation back in Switzerland, but the British Police had decided not to press any charges within the UK.

'You are very fortunate, young lady. The British authorities have been very understanding and have been informed that your mother and daughter have been found and are safe and well. We will be flying home to Switzerland with you tomorrow where you will each receive further treatment in a Swiss hospital. The Swiss Police and Customs have said they will wish to interview you, but at least you can be reunited with your family,' he said.

Ursula asked if she could visit Peter before leaving the hospital.

'I will speak to the senior doctor, but I'm sure a brief visit will be in order. I understand the young British journalist owes you a special thank you for what you did on his behalf at Interlaken. He could well have been killed had it not been for your intervention,' said the diplomat with a smile.

Back in Peter's room in intensive care, a consultant was taking a further look at his patient. 'I think in two or three days you can leave the hospital, but I strongly recommend several weeks of recuperation. Nothing too strenuous,' he said with a twinkle in his eye. 'But perhaps I can recommend a quiet stay in a hotel here in the Scottish Highlands. Nice views, some gentle walks and good nourishing food to build you up again,' he added.

Sue asked him if he could recommend a particular hotel.

'Not really, as we have so many nice Scottish hotels here in the Highlands. But I live about forty-five minutes from this hospital in a delightful village called Loch Awe. It is alongside a loch and there is a super three-star hotel of the same name at the village. It was designed to look like a castle and even has its own railway station,' he said.

'That sounds delightful,' said Sue to Peter. 'It could prove really romantic, Peter.'

Peter saw the smile and guessed what Sue really had in mind, which was strange because he had similar thoughts, but he wouldn't tell Sue until they were at the hotel.

As his memory started returning, Peter couldn't believe all that had happened since leaving for Austria with Sue the week before Christmas. He had been mistaken for someone else, kidnapped, shot; he had been drugged and then nearly died in a plane crash. *What a story*, he thought. But that was for another day. The real story unfolding was his love for Sue. Several weeks at the Loch Awe Hotel being pampered and loved by such a beautiful girl could only happen in a book!

Or could it?